Lions

WINNING!

"That horse has a great future," said Jamie.

"Well I hope you'll ride him again," said Ben.

"Just try and stop me," replied Jamie, smiling at me with his wide, lazy smile which made a shiver of excitement run up my spine. That day, we all felt we were in at the beginning of something special.

GINNY ELLIOT

WINNING!

Lions
A Division of HarperCollins*Publishers*

First published in Great Britain in Lions in 1995
1 3 5 7 9 8 6 4 2

Lions is an imprint of CollinsChildren'sBooks,
a division of HarperCollins Publishers Ltd,
77-85 Fulham Palace Road, Hammersmith,
London W6 8JB

Copyright © Virginia Elliot 1995

ISBN 0 00 675036 2

The author asserts the moral right to be identified
as the author of the work.

Printed and bound in Great Britain
by HarperCollins Manufacturing Ltd, Glasgow

For my husband, Mikey –
who does indeed have 'the patience of Job'!
With love and thanks for putting up with
my endless questions about the plot
and angsting over the story!

And special thanks to my mother,
Heather Holgate, and Dorothy Willis,
who have encouraged and supported me in
my riding career and shared my lifelong
enthusiasm for horses, which provides
the inspiration behind this book.

CHAPTER ONE

"A new horse!"

When I strolled into the yard and saw Ben leaning against the fence watching a big, stocky chestnut running in the paddock, I got such a surprise that I switched off my Walkman – and it takes a lot to make me do that.

"I know, Becky, I know, I promised the Governor the next thing we bought would be a new kitchen," said Ben, throwing up his hands in mock surrender when he saw me. "But I picked him up really cheap. I suppose you could say he's an ugly looking brute."

He was a big chestnut, with a small white blaze and one white hind sock, about 16'3 hands high, with very large ears. I would soon get to know his habit of cocking one ear on one side, with the other ear forward, as if he was using his own special kind of radar.

"He's got good bone, though," went on Ben, "and he may be a lanky six-year-old now, but you wait until he matures and becomes more muscled up across his topline."

"He's a cracker," I replied. "Where did you get him?"

"I bought him from a Mrs Peak – he literally carted her out hunting and she was pretty terrified a couple of times, which is why she decided to sell him. She'd bred him, and was keen to hang on to him, but she just couldn't afford to put him into training."

Ben paused and scratched his head with the pencil that was always stuck through his dark curly hair.

"But I got a feeling about this one. He's got these big ears set on that wonderful, big head for a purpose. You wait – soon there'll be no stopping him. He's the nearest I've seen to those old-fashioned steeplechasers."

By this time, I was so desperate to ride him that I was practically salivating. But Ben would have none of it.

"Let him settle in a bit, first," said Ben. "Just now he looks like a fighting cockerel. And you don't want to end up by being frightened off – like poor old Mrs Peak.

I snorted: "As if I would be!"

Ben ignored this intellectual argument and gave me a pleading look. "I'd be grateful if you had a word with the Governor, Becky," he said. "It's not only this here horse that needs calming down."

I found the Governor – that's what we call Ben's wife, Sue – in the kitchen. She looked her usual lovable, messy self, in a huge sweatshirt and baggy cord trousers.

When I was off school last term with some flu bug, I found myself watching day-time TV. Well, it was either that or some GCSE course work – and I saw a woman making scones. She'd explained how you needed cool hands and a light touch. Sue was making scones at the kitchen table, but her cheeks were flushed, and the way she was

9

throwing the dough about, I thought she'd probably end up with rock cakes.

"Have you seen it?" Sue asked glumly. "That's our new kitchen cantering round the paddock."

I looked round the kitchen that I knew as well as my own – at all the surfaces covered in familiar tins and mugs and the worn linoleum on the floor. I'd been coming over to Ben and Sue Mainwaring's since before I could remember. Beside the huge butler's sink were containers for foil, vegetable scraps etc. Sue was an ace recycler, and the way she looked just now I thought she would cheerfully have recycled Ben.

"Come on, Sue," I said, "you hate cooking really."

"Don't tell me you're on Ben's side, Becky," she said. "You two are double trouble. Look in there," she went on, tossing me a glossy magazine with floury hands. "I was looking for ideas, and apparently 'farmhouse kitchens' are all the rage. Well, I can tell them how to achieve that 'distressed' look," she added, kicking the old range. "You simply don't decorate for ten years and get people to walk through with cow pat on their boots every half hour."

I passed Ben on my way out and gave him a jokey warning, "I should duck on your way in. The Governor's on the rampage."

Ben grimaced, "Thanks for telling me! Becky, I've put you down for a quiet hack on the new horse tomorrow."

"Terrific! Does he have a name yet?"

"Mrs Peak called him some wet name like Conkers – very imaginative with him being a chestnut. But we'll have to come up with something better – more suited to the winners' enclosure at Aintree, say."

I looked back at the horse in the paddock and he cocked his ears in that funny distinctive way he had, as if he was sending me a signal. I received it loud and clear – could he be what I had been waiting for – something really special that I could work with and bring out the best in. And him in me?

When I tell people I live with my grandfather, I can see them thinking that it must be really boring living with an old fogey, and going home to warm milk and slippers and a nice game of dominoes.

But Ned – I can't imagine calling him Grandpa! – is really more of a mate. He was in the SAS and used to play polo and wouldn't know a domino if one turned up in his gin and tonic.

When he was younger, he looked incredibly dashing – all jodhpurs and linen shirts, like something out of a Merchant Ivory film. He's travelled all over the world and knows anyone who's anyone. Some VIP who's the Sultan of somewhere or other, met Ned at Sandhurst, sponsored him and paid for his polo ponies. It strikes me that if you're as talented and handsome as Ned, you'll always get someone to sponsor you.

Anyway, my parents were killed in a car crash when I was only two. I don't remember them, and one thing Ned taught me is that playing the poor orphan will get me nowhere.

Ned was pulling up in our old landrover when I came up the drive.

"The Mainwarings have got a great new horse and I'm going to help school him," I called.

"And what about *your* schooling?" Ned shouted back. "Your GCSEs are coming up soon. I don't want another argument about you leaving school after them and being a trainer – there's no money in it. Why don't you stay on and become a vet?"

"Because I don't want to spend my life with my hand up cows'—" I checked myself, and then said. "I only want to work with horses."

"Lunch is in the Aga," said Ned, closing a well–worn argument.

I went in, with Shelley, the sheepdog who makes up our family, at my heels.

"The Mainwarings have got a new horse and it's going to be a champion and *I'm* going to be a famous trainer," I said out loud. (I tell Shelley looked at me quizzically – there I was talking to myself again!

Lunch was a casserole of pigeons in a

dark, rich gravy, followed by a chewy walnut tart. That's another thing about Ned – he loves cooking. Lots of my friends live on hamburgers and spaghetti hoops, and when I go to their houses for tea it's a toss–up between what would be better to eat – the frozen gateau or the box it came in. In fact I have to tell Ned to tone it down a bit when friends come here. It's embarrassing giving people *boeuf bourguignon* and baked Alaska when they're expecting beans on toast.

I did all my homework that afternoon, so I could rush off first thing on Sunday.

Once I'd finished, I phoned my friend, Chrissie. I told Ned, who'd been complaining about the phone bills, that I wanted to pick her brains about the French revolution, for a history essay. But in fact it was something much more important – I was desperate to know how her haircut had gone, and to tell her about the chestnut.

"You're mad!" she said, when I told her. "You're the only person I know who'd rather muck out a stable than go to a film or go shopping."

I didn't tell her the last time she'd dragged me round the shops – in search of the perfect pair of black boots – I'd felt as exhausted as if I'd mucked out ten stables.

That night I dreamt I was trying to jump the new chestnut over a fence but he would not budge. We were rooted to the spot. When I woke up, I found that Shelley had gone to sleep on my bed and was lying like a dead weight over my legs.

The Governor seemed in a better mood on Sunday morning; perhaps it was the weather. Sun was streaming down on the farmhouse. It's buildings are higgledy-piggledy, with a cow milking unit at one end and twelve loose boxes made out of old barns and outhouses. But don't let that deceive you – it's incredibly organised and well run.

I've seen smart yards, with gravel drives and rose gardens in the middle and acres of Eurotrack gallops for their precious horses to run on in all weathers. Sue tries her best, with flower baskets here and there, but it's all done on a shoestring. And it's a lot of work – the've turned a couple of their grass pasture fields into their gallops, and, because it's turf, it's got to be really nurtured and cared for.

I know Ben would give his eye teeth for a horsewalker – that's a circular bit of machinery which is used when horses come back from work. You can get about eight horses on it at a time and it walks them dry after they've been worked to avoid the horses getting chilled. It's a great timesaver for staff.

'Staff' to the Mainwarings is one lad, called John, who helps Ben and Sue with the milking and their two point-to-pointers and now, of course, the new horse.

"What kept you?" asked Sue. The milking was over and she was sitting at the kitchen table writing in the yield book. "Off you go – and don't forget your crash hat."

Ben used to ride in point-to-points in the days when he was much less chunky. These days he usually rode the big coloured horse, Brian, but he's desperate to stay in racing and

I know he sees this new horse as his best chance yet.

He was walking the gelding on a long lunge line when I arrived.

"I'm just letting him get the feel of his new home before I saddle him up. He's been holidaying for three months since the hunting season finished."

"I'll be really careful," I said. "Just a gentle hack."

I was itching to get my hands on him and ride out. It was ideal weather – as far as I'm concerned, you can keep spring. Give me autumn, with its bonfirey smells and Christmas just around the corner.

"I want you to take him very gently, just on the path round the farm. No fields yet," said Ben. "I was thinking of coming with you on Brian," he added, "but it's probably better if it's just the two of you. The big brute might be too much of a distraction."

I went into the tack room. It always reminds me of a gypsy caravan in there, with rugs, saddles, bridles and boots all jumbled in together. It's warm, because there's a

Rayburn stove, which comes in handy for boiling up barley for horses that need to put on a bit of weight. All right, so it's not huge with central heating and a proper drying room with a washing machine and everything, but I like it.

When I was tacking the chestnut up, he put his ears back, and his teeth went smack, hard together, as if he was going to nip me. I soon found out that this was his way of teasing me, and luckily his teeth always stopped two inches short of my elbow – or my bum – or else there wouldn't be much left of me by now.

"Conkers indeed!" I said. "You're a right Monkey."

I had persuaded Ben to let me hack out in a racing saddle. To be honest, I'm not that used to them, but I'm fed up with normal saddles with long stirrups. Very pony club!

We walked out of the farmyard. In theory, I knew that I should stay walking, but I just couldn't resist having a short trot. I felt the tremendous spring in him, and itched to get him on the gallops.

"I suppose we'd better be getting back," I said at last. "We can circle round and go in by the back gate."

By now, I was getting the feel of him. He just seemed to glide across the ground, and it was the unseen extraordinary action in his hind legs that propelled us forward. He was easily the most active horse I'd ever been on.

He had a very good sloping shoulder – known in the trade as a 'good front' – which meant he seemed to float across the top of the ground. Ben had also pointed out how much bone he had – "nine inches of bone" – as he put it. He meant his legs were in good proportion to his body so, with any luck, he would stand up well to the rigours of racing.

I was feeling quite pleased with myself, not least because I'd managed to stay in the racing saddle, which I must admit I was finding extremely odd with its short stirrups. I was thinking about what Ned had said when I'd first started riding:

"You've got your mother's seat." Then he'd added, "A large bottom!" I was mortified, but he went on, "No, really – you've got a wonderful natural position and balance."

I started laughing at the memory, but then something happened that wiped the smile right off my face,

The horse cocked its ears to the side, and its body stiffened. A split second later I heard the sound of hooves beating on hard earth and an unearthly, guttural noise like a foghorn.

Straight across our path thundered a huge, black bull, its eyes blank and staring. It missed us by barely a metre and crashed through the opposite hedge as easily as if it were cotton wool.

The chestnut halted, hesitated for a moment, and then broke into a flat-out gallop, racing like the wind down the path. I felt a surge of unleashed power and knew I'd lost control. I was terrified. I hung on, my heart thumping, talking to myself, saying, "Stay calm, Becky, just sit tight."

There was a fence straight ahead. I tried to slow the horse down, but he galloped as if possessed, floating above the ground. My mind blanked in sheer panic, and I had no idea if we were going to make it. But the chestnut took control, and his powerful hind quarters came into their own.

We soared over the fence, and I felt a surge of relief, my body relaxing as we thundered to the ground the other side. I was trembling all over as I managed to take control, then cantered a few paces down the path. We trotted a bit to calm down and then I dismounted.

"You gave me a fright there, Monkey," I said in his ear, and he nipped at the air beside my neck.

Back at the farm, Sue came rushing over as soon as she saw us, shouting, "Thank God! We've been frantic. Glendower's broken loose and he's on the rampage. Thinks he's a wretched racehorse, not a bull!"

"He gave us a bit of a fright," I said. "But did anyone see us jumping the fence up there?"

"Jumping?" said Ben, coming ove., "I thought I said a gentle hack."

"Well your new horse had other ideas," I said, still panting from the exhilaration.

I took the chestnut to the stable and rubbed him down. He stood there as quiet as a lamb.

"You can't fool me, Monkey," I said. "I've seen just how powerful you are. For the moment, let's keep this our secret."

When he was safely stabled, I wandered into the kitchen. I still felt a bit shaky and Sue gave me a worried look.

"I'm going to ring Ned and ask him over to supper," she said. "I think we could all do with a relaxing evening. Although the grub won't be up to Ned's standards."

"That'll be brilliant, Governor," said Ben, putting his arm round her, affectionately. "I'll get out some of that special claret."

Suddenly I noticed they both looked quite tired and I had a brainwave.

"Why don't we have fish and chips – out of the paper, with a glass of wine. Ned would love it."

"Well, that would give me time to catch up on things," said Sue. "I could even have a long soak later and change out of these old cords."

"Into slightly newer cords?" said Ben. Clothes were at the very bottom of Sue's list of priorities.

Later, Ned and I drove over and Ben went out for fish and chips. Sue had put candles on the dining table, and Ben had fetched some good claret and crystal glasses, but we all insisted we wanted to eat the fish and chips out of the paper.

"It doesn't taste the same, otherwise," agreed Ned.

When Ben came back he passed the steaming parcels round the table. Mine was wrapped in the *Racing Post* – well, this is a racing area, I suppose. I'd had a glass of wine, and I was just tearing off a piece of plaice, when I saw the most amazing face. He looked about nineteen, and had a lazy smile and black hair falling over his forehead. The paper was damp with vinegar, but I managed to read beneath the photo: Jamie Howland, who seems to go from strength to strength, collects his Champion Jockey award.

I felt my stomach contract as I looked at the picture. Chrissie's always banging on about fancying the man of the moment, but I had honestly never felt that way myself. I preferred racing up the gallops to hanging about smoky discos. But when I looked at Jamie's picture, I suddenly knew exactly what she meant. He looked almost edible. I was just wondering if I could do with a new haircut, when Ben broke in on my thoughts.

"You'll be glad to know Glendower's back in his stall," he was saying, "with a new chain that the *Queen Mary* couldn't break."

"*Queen Mary*, eh?" said Sue. "That dates you!"

"I shudder every time I think about Glendower. Becky and that horse could have been like a red rag to him."

"You know, that's not half bad," said Ned.

"Mmm, the chips are hardly soggy at all," mumbled Sue through her mouthful.

"Not that," said Ned, "I'm thinking about a name for a prize steeplechaser. How does Red Rag sound?"

"Trust you," said Ben, filling up Ned's

glass. He filled mine up too, and no one said anything. The others were drinking the claret as if it was coke, and it was decided that we would stay the night in the spare bedrooms that were littered through the rambling old farmhouse.

I remember that evening as a warm, glowing scene, like when I was small and used to look through red cellophane toffee paper. Ned told some of his best polo stories and everyone toasted everyone else, and then we all toasted Red Rag.

"And Jamie Howland," I added, just under my breath.

CHAPTER TWO

Soon it felt as if he had lived at the farm in Wantage all his life. Ben was right. His body did catch up with his large head until he looked noble and handsome rather than ungainly.

I felt the knowledge I had picked up at pony club was really stretched when I came to school him, and so I devoured any training books I could get my hands on. He loved to jump, but he would take terrible risks because he had no idea about technique.

"You must admit, he is a natural jumper," I said to Ben one day.

"But he still has to learn discipline, and to take command," said Ben, firmly.

I still rode out every morning with Ben

and Sue and their other horses, but I spent more and more time in the paddock, schooling Red Rag. I know now that there are no short cuts to training a horse. Ben had always drilled it into me:

"Prevention is better than cure – the easiest way to wipe out bad habits, girl, is to stop them starting."

A lot of people forget that training is a two-way partnership, and if a horse is not progressing, it's a good idea to check you're not doing anything wrong yourself.

"Remember to think of yourself like a tree," said Ben, when I started training Red Rag.

I wondered, at first, if he'd had a nip of rum to keep out the cold and got carried away, but then he explained.

"Your arms and legs – the branches and roots – must be able to move independently of each other, while your body – the trunk – remains still. And it's your weight, not your seat, that you use as an aid to control the horse. There's a lot of rot talked about seats," went on Ben, who's not one to beat about the bush – or tree.

I thought Red Rag was getting better looking by the day, but Ben said, "Handsome is as handsome does. What's the best thing about him, d'you think?"

"His sloping shoulders and his lean withers? His temperament? His strength?" I said, sounding like a check-list in a training manual.

"I'll tell you what's the best thing," said Ben. "He *enjoys* moving and he loves jumping. It's been bred in him, and it's just up to us to encourage it and bring it out."

It wasn't long before I tried Red Rag over trotting poles on the ground. I started with one pole and quietly lunged him at walk, adding more poles gradually and adjusting them to fit in with his footfalls. After about two weeks, he was trotting over six poles, laid out in a fan–shaped curve.

Ben showed me how to place the poles just a little further apart each time, to encourage Red Rag to lengthen his stride. He seemed to know by eye, and experience, just where to put them, and I longed for the day when it would all be second nature to me, too. I found it really hard to be patient all the time.

"Can't we raise the poles on blocks today?" I asked every day, but it wasn't until Ben was sure the horse had hit his natural and best stride, that we put blocks under the poles. I thought Ben was being too cautious. "You didn't see him jump that huge fence," I wailed. "I did."

"We're building in good habits gradually," said Ben, as Red Rag trotted happily over the raised poles. "He's getting to trust us – look at how loose and easy his back and shoulders are."

Deep down, I knew Ben was right. I was desperate to ride Red Rag but lessons on the lunge are a very important grounding, and there are no short cuts (he's got me saying it now!).

Lungeing is like being part of a triangle, made up of the lunge line, the horse, and the person holding the whip. You can widen or close up the triangle by putting the whip closer to the horse's hocks or further away.

It's really the first step in teaching a horse to concentrate and make an effort.

The lunge line is fed out so that the horse moves away from the trainer – in this case, me! – and on to a circle at a walk. At this stage, Red Rag was kitted out in cavesson, with a lunge rein attached to a front ring, and had boots on all his legs.

About two days after this, Red Rag, who was walking in a very controlled, obedient way, was allowed to trot. The tack was built up gradually: a saddle and girths, then stirrups which were gradually lengthened, then bridle, reins and finally side-reins which were eventually shortened.

Ben wrote down some golden rules for me, and I pinned them up on my bedroom wall and memorised them. Even now, if I close my eyes I can see the words in red felt tip:

We want the horse to learn to:
> go forward
> stay in rhythm
> accept contact on both reins
> balance himself with the weight of

> the rider
>
> be straight
>
> maintain the correct bend.

We were able to focus all this attention on Red Rag because the Mainwairings didn't have many other horses in the yard at the time and, of course, I had made him my special project. I stuck these pointers up on my pinboard, next to the rather blurred, vinegar-stained picture of Jamie Howland I'd surreptitiously cut from the *Racing Post.*

Chrissie studied these two new additions the next time she was over, and said, "I see, is that what you'd like this rather hunky-looking guy to do, then? Maybe there is something in this riding game, after all."

"Chrissie," I said scornfully, "there are no short cuts."

It was bliss when I could finally mount Red Rag and jump small jumps. I wasn't worried at all about height at this stage – just laying down good habits and, most important of all, staying straight. After all, what good is it if you can jump huge fences, but all askew? It could be nasty!

After three weeks, we were jumping a grid of four fences of almost a metre from trot. I literally gave Red Rag his head – dropping the reins and letting him use his full, stretched power by freeing his head and neck.

After each session ("Keep them short!" – Ben) I talked to him and encouraged him: "Well done, Monkey. Slow and steady does it." I knew he was getting used to my voice, just as much as my weight on his back.

Ben often came into the paddock to see how I was doing. He was impressed to see how straight we were going.

"Move to the right or the left on a course, and you'll lose ground, because you'll lose length," he said, running his hands through his unruly hair in his enthusiasm.

As Red Rag settled in, his true nature came out. He was no angel. One morning I arrived at the yard to find that he had undone the bolts of his door with his teeth. Not content with his own bid for freedom, he'd opened the other stable doors as well, and let out the other horses. Luckily, they hadn't bolted or anything, but had just pootered about the yard until John led them firmly back.

Another trick he had was as soon as I put his water bucket down in his stable – nine times out of ten he'd knock it over and get the straw in his box all wet. I never worked out how much of this was deliberate. And why did a horse which had such immaculate control during grid work, always manage to stand on my toe when I was grooming him?

"Monkey, you're driving me absolutely nuts. Stand still!" I'd yell at him.

After about six weeks, Red Rag was doing two-by-two miles at 545 metres a minute up the gallops. As his first race loomed, I had settled him into a weekly routine and had managed to follow Ben's advice about keeping the sessions short. When I wasn't riding Red Rag, or helping with the other horses, I was usually curled up with an apple and a training manual, trying to pick up tips.

Ben knew lots of tricks. One day he laid a circle of sawdust on the ground and told me to ride Red Rag around it.

"If you control him properly," he said,

"the sawdust will be picked up by his feet at every turn."

But the hardest thing of all, was keeping the schooling to short sessions. Time passed so quickly, I could never believe that I'd been on horseback for fifteen or twenty minutes. I always took time to tell Red Rag how well he'd worked and his confidence grew to match his grown body.

"I think we're ready for our first trial over the schooling fences," said Ben one morning.

I rode Red Rag, and Sue joined me on Venus, a grey. Venus knew the territory well, and was there to help give the new horse confidence. We were to do the gallops upsides.

Alongside the gallops lay the schooling fences. These would help give Red Rag his first taste of the procedure at a race meeting.

I was really nervous. How would the chestnut react? Would he be as brilliant as I hoped? Red Rag hesitated and I patted his neck to soothe him before we set off.

I remembered Ben's advice always to look straight ahead between his ears, keep him pushed up to the bit and in good balance.

With each jump he seemed to grow in confidence and by the end of the line, it felt as if he had been doing it all his life.

Ben had watched it all from afar, and when we returned, he said confidently, "I reckon, with a lot of practice, it won't be long before his first novice chase."

"Hurdling?" said Sue.

"Not him," said Ben. "No, he'll go straight into novice chase – it's what he's made for."

I couldn't think of anything except Red Rag's first race now. Ned began to notice that I was spending a lot of time with my text books open at the kitchen table, staring out of the window. Then one day he found I'd doodled a pair of double jumps in the margin of my maths exercise book.

"Look," he said, "you're always telling me how clever that horse is. I don't expect it wants to go around with an ignoramus on its back. As far as I know there aren't any GCSEs in hacking – or football."

Football was my other passion. I hate it when Ned's sarcastic. So I pulled my socks up and made sure Ned had no cause to complain, because I was terrified in case he said I couldn't go along for Red Rag's début.

"We've got to a new Shakespeare play in English," I said very casually one supper time, "and I'm keeping it in case I'm bored in the box."

"Box?" said Ned, looking up from dishing up some seafood lasagne. "What box?"

"Box?" barked Shelley, who often echoed Ned when he thought he was saying something interesting.

"The box that's taking Red Rag to Wincanton on Saturday," I said. "I'm sure I told you about it," I added. Actually I was sure I hadn't and I could feel myself blushing and knew that all my freckles would be joining up in that annoying way. Would I never grow out of it?

"I think I'd better have a word with Ben," said Ned.

"We reckon Red Rag's ready for his first novice chase – and Wincanton's one of what I think of as one of those flat and easy courses – although the fences are quite stiff," said Ben when Ned rang him up. "Becky'll be quite safe – I'm going to drive the horsebox myself."

"And I have to tell the jockey all about Red Rag, and how to get the best out of him," I added at Ned's elbow.

It was agreed that I could travel with Red Rag, and I began a tough programme of canter work-outs and fitness work. He seemed to know the length of his own stride by instinct and judged the distance he needed to be from a fence when he made his spring as if it had been worked out on a computer.

The six days leading up to the race went like this: **Sunday,** rest day; **Monday,** one-and-a-half hour hack, and lungeing; **Tuesday,** two-by-two miles up the gallops (Tuesday was my favourite day); **Wednesday,** one-and-a-half hour hack and some light lungeing (it can't be all thrills); **Thursday,** riding over hills and a few jumps; **Friday,** a one-and-a-half hour hack – and a canter workout to get my Monkey in the mood and give him the right sort of dreams.

All the patient training had led up to his

first novice chase.

The afternoon before the race, I was grooming him. I moved closer to him, talking to myself as much as him, and I said, "This is it, Monkey. This is your chance to show us all what you're made of. *I* know you're a star, and all these people tomorrow are going to see it for themselves."

He moved his ears, signalling to me as if he'd spoken, "Message received and understood."

CHAPTER THREE

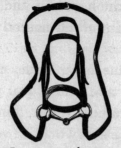

The next day I was awake at what Ben calls sparrowfart, my stomach tense with excitement. Ned stumbled down to the kitchen in his old Viyella dressing gown, to find me staring out of the window, watching the dawn break. He made a pot of tea and we sat down at the kitchen table. I felt I should apologise for being so bolshie over the past few days. I knew that I'd been behaving badly.

"Ned..." I began.

But he knew me too well. I didn't need to put it into words. He could see that I was so tense, I would easily tip over the edge. In fact, he did the best possible thing, which was to ask me a lot of technical details about Red Rag.

"It's such a fine balance between instilling discipline in the horse," I said, "and at the same time letting all his natural power come out."

We had some lovely horsey chit-chat, and Ned laughed and said, "You really know what you're talking about, don't you? You know, your parents would be very proud of you, Becky."

"Oh, rubbish," I said, and rushed off to have a bath, but it pleased me just the same.

When I left the cottage, Ned called after me, "Remember, I've put all your allowance for the next six months on that damned horse."

I gave Red Rag his feed and began to groom him to within an inch of his life, plaiting him up three times to get it just right.

"Don't let me down now, Monkey," I said to him.

"Right, lass," said Ben, coming into the stable, "I've been on the phone to O'Leary and he'll see us at the course a good hour beforehand so you can tell him all Red Rag's little ways."

I told myself for the hundredth time that Patrick O'Leary was a jockey that everyone trusted, and the butterflies in my stomach changed the rhythm of their dance a little.

"I've made an extra fruit cake for O'Leary," said Sue, popping out of the kitchen with a hamper, "but tell him not to touch it till after the race. Goodness knows how many pounds he'd put on. I've checked that these will fit him," she went on, smoothing a pile of shimmering blue and grey owner's colours between sheets of tissue paper. "Be sure and give them to a valet as soon as you arrive."

We packed everything in the horsebox and Sue came to help prepare Red Rag.

"You do know your sweater's inside out?" I said to her. "Is that for luck, or is it a new fashion?"

"Oh heavens," she said, looking down at her ample front, "I was up so early I dressed in the dark – and I'm so excited I didn't even notice."

Red Rag's feed had been an hour earlier than usual, and he knew something special was happening. We slipped on his headcollar, with a rope attached to tether him securely, and put on his long travelling boots, which were shaped to cover and protect part of his knees and hocks.

I had already bandaged his tail, so I led him gently up the ramp and tied him up and then climbed up into the passenger seat beside Ben.

I'd been to a few race meetings with Ben, but this was special. I wasn't just one of the milling throng, I was going to go into the parade paddock ring, and as I looked round I felt as if the whole place had been designed specially for me. At the gates, there was the usual smell of jellied eels and the newspaper sellers shouting words that were impossible to understand.

Ben parked the horsebox and went off to the Clerk of the Course's office to declare Red Rag and officially enter him for his race. In the weighing room, he met O'Leary and passed the racing silks over to a valet. In the changing rooms, he said there were only three valets to look after about forty jockeys, and it felt like complete chaos. I had to take his word for it because, being a girl, I had more chance of getting into Fort Knox. That hadn't stopped me having the odd fantasy, which I'd shared with Chrissie, of helping Jamie Howland change out of his racing gear.

"Wouldn't you feel odd, rubbing down something with only two legs?" said Chrissie. She thinks she's got a sense of humour.

O'Leary gathered up all his paraphernalia and went off to be weighed. I knew that the Clerk of the Scales sat beside them in a chair beside a clock face marked in pounds. The Judge also sat nearby, studying the colours each jockey wore, so that in a close finish he would know which horse was which very quickly, without waiting for the photo-finish pictures.

When he was weighed, O'Leary handed the saddle to Ben, who took it off to the saddling boxes close to the parade ring to saddle up Red Rag. Soon, I saw O'Leary come rushing up to meet Red Rag for himself.

"So it's your first race, my friend," he said in his soft Irish brogue, and Red Rag's ears swung up. Here was someone who knew all about horses.

"Well, we'll not start you off on the inside, you'll have enough to cope with without worrying about being pushed to the side by some big brute.

"What about blinkers?" He turned to Ben.

"You don't understand," I butted in. "Nothing unsettles this horse. He'll just want to sail over those fences."

But O'Leary just looked through me as if I were a bale of hay, and carried on talking about Red Rag to Ben.

"You wait," I said to myself, "I'll show you I know a thing or two about horses."

"Time to see for ourselves," said O'Leary, as Ben legged him up into the saddle and he checked his girths. Then they cantered down to the first fence, to show the horses their task, and cantered back to the start.

The Starter called a roll to make sure everyone had arrived, and the jockeys circled round at the starting point. I could feel the blood rushing in my ears as the horses lined up and I dashed off with Ben to find the best position to watch the race, and within sight of the finishing line. Then the tape flew up, the horses raced off and Red Rag was on his way to his first jump.

At once he streaked ahead, out in front with three other horses. Every time Red Rag heard hoofbeats at his quarters, he put on a fresh spurt until he was two lengths in front and only two jumps remained.

"I see," O'Leary was thinking – as he told me later. "You like to lead from the front, do you, but will you have anything in reserve?"

I grabbed Ben's arm when I saw him thundering up to the last fence – he showed me later where the soft tweed of his jacket was all mangled.

"He's racing as if Glendower's at his back," I breathed. "I can't watch the last fence!" But I couldn't take my eyes off him. "Come on, Monkey," I said, under my breath, digging my nails into my palms.

"He's not going to change tack now, lass," said Ben. "He's got the smell of victory in his nostrils."

Sure enough, Red Rag flew over the last fence as if it were a dandelion in his path, with the natural pacing that meant he saved vital seconds on hesitating or adjusting his stride. His hooves beat against the green track and I felt my heartbeat speeding up to keep time.

In the end, he won by three clear lengths. I threw my arms round Ben and hugged him. He lifted me right off the ground and I wouldn't have been surprised if he'd thrown me up in the air. The only thing that brought me down to earth was the sight of the vet's van speeding off to a horse that had fallen at the fifth fence.

"We did it, Ben!" I said at last. "He's a

winner. If he won here, there's no reason why he shouldn't go on and on, and win – every-thing!"

"Come on, stop chattering" said Ben, tak-ing me by the arm and leading me out of the stand. For some strange reason, I had started to shake all over.

"Well, you were right, after all," laughed O'Leary when we caught up with him in the winners' enclosure. I was still a bit miffed at his dismissive treatment of me, but when he added, "You've got a potential champion there, you know," I couldn't stop myself beaming at him.

"I hardly needed to do anything at all," said O'Leary, "just sit on there and let him do what he knew best." He left, smiling, to weigh in.

"You know you've earned a chunk of the prize money," said Ben. "All that work you put into schooling Red Rag paid off."

I could feel that annoying blush starting again, and I was about to refuse it. But then I thought how nice it would be to be able to give Ned something. Perhaps I could even take him out for a meal, although I knew he would only criticise the food very loudly. But then I caught sight of myself on the side of a shiny metal van, and I thought, No, to Hell with food, what I need is a decent haircut and some new clothes.

Ned was waiting at the farm with Sue. Shelley rushed up to the horsebox, barking joyfully.

"Well done!" shouted Sue as Red Rag was led gently down the ramp. "I think there'll be a special feed for you." Her voice was a bit trembly and she was wearing blue eye shadow on one eye, and green eye shadow on the other. She'd obviously made a very unusual attempt at make-up to welcome us home, but as usual, the results were haphazard.

"And for you two," she added. "Ned's brought over something for supper."

I settled Red Rag in his stable. "We showed them," I whispered in his ear. "There's no stopping you now, Monkey."

In the kitchen, Sue was taking a pie out of the oven.

"There's cider – not Champagne," said

Ned. "I didn't want to tempt fate."

"Well I'm going to do just that," said Ben, draining a glass of cider. "I'm going to say that that horse out there is a winner. A few more novice chases to give him a bit of experience, like, and I'd say we're looking at a Gold Cup horse."

"The Gold Cup at Cheltenham?" I asked, stupidly, because what other one is there?

"That's the one," said Ben, "but it'll mean a lot of work."

"I'll help all I can," I said. "Just think – we have our very own Gold Cup horse in the making."

And to myself, I added, "I know my schooling made all the difference. I know I've got a real knack, and there's no reason on earth why I shouldn't be a famous trainer." Suddenly, everything seemed possible, and I felt as if I was soaring over the last fence of my childhood and galloping into the grown-up world.

On the drive home, Ned thought I was quiet because I was so tired. I was tired but my mind was very active. I kept asking myself if, now that Red Rag was proving himself, he would be an attractive proposition for a champion jockey. Especially one called Jamie. It all depended, I knew, on the next few races.

CHAPTER FOUR

I needn't have worried. Red Rag went on to win all four of his novice chases, and Ben entered him for the Sun Alliance Novice Chase at Cheltenham.

By now, I felt I had really got under his skin and knew his responses almost as well as my own. I tried to explain my feelings to Chrissie, but she just said, "Oh yeah, and if it was a choice between a night out with Red Duster or whatever it's called, or Tom Cruise, which would you choose?"

It was the first time Ben had had a horse running at Cheltenham, and his excitement was infectious.

"D'you think I could borrow some money for a new outfit, to wear to Cheltenham?" I asked Ned.

"Why worry about clothes? As long as you're clean and tidy," he said. "You've got good bones, and lovely teeth – and that's what really matters."

He made me sound like a horse. Red Rag was luckier. The Governor bought him an amazing new paddock parade rug with B.M. for Ben Mainwaring on the corner.

"I thought you were saving up for a new kitchen," I said, as Sue tried it on Red Rag in his stable.

"Oh come off it," she said. "Next thing you'll be saying we should have called the horse 'Fitted Unit'."

It was a blowy spring morning, and I was helping John muck out. I had tumbled out of bed and pulled on old jeans and a sweatshirt and rushed over without even brushing my hair. Well, you don't dress up to muck out, do you?

I came out of a stable with a shovelful of old straw and the wind blew some of it back in my face and a few strands got caught in my hair. So when Ben called, "Becky, here's someone I'd like you to meet," I imagine I looked like Wurzel Gummidge.

In the middle of the yard, in jeans and a blue denim shirt that matched the colour of his eyes exactly, stood Jamie Howland. I was so surprised I nearly dropped the shovel. My stomach lurched and I felt as if I was jumping a very high fence.

"Jamie's come to give Red Rag the once over," said Ben. "He's going to take him over the schooling fences."

I knew that Jamie Howland only ever rode horses that he felt had great potential, and the Gold Cup seemed suddenly that bit closer.

"This is Becky, who's schooled Red Rag since the day he arrived," said Ben.

"I taught him everything he knows," I said brightly. But Jamie just looked dismissively at me as if to say, "Sorry, only two legs and no withers. Not interested."

"D'you fancy a bacon roll before you try Red Rag for yourself?" asked Ben, and I expected Jamie to say, like most jockeys, "I only eat spinach and steamed fish with the odd glass of lemon and water." But he went off to the kitchen door and appeared soon afterwards, leaning against the lintel, demolishing a huge floury roll with bacon sticking out all round it.

I passed him on my way in and I couldn't resist saying, "It's awful how you jockeys have to starve yourselves, isn't it?" But he just chewed more noisily.

He was one of those magic people who can eat what they like without putting on weight. And wear old jeans and denim shirts and make them look as if they're designer clothes. But his main magic was kept for horses.

He rode out on Red Rag quite a few times that spring, and he seemed able to tap into the horse's potential and bring out the best in him. I watched him riding, looking for the key, but it all looked quite effortless.

I made a bit of an effort not to look as if I'd been dragged through a ditch when I was over at the yard. But every time I bumped into Jamie I seemed to be just coming from some dirty job and covered in sweat and smuts. He never seemed to notice me and I heard on the grapevine that the cottage he rented in Lambourne was besieged night and day by glamorous blondes. I raided Boots make-up counter, and tried to cover my freckles with blusher, but the only response came from Ned, who said, "Are you sickening for something? You look a bit flushed."

Anyway, Jamie liked what he saw in Red Rag, at least, and he agreed to ride him in the Sun Alliance.

March came in as fierce and snarling as the MGM lion and the wind whistled round the Mainwaring's old farmhouse. Sue's kitchen brochures gathered dust in a corner, while she pored over the *Racing Post* and studied the form of the other horses.

"What are you going to wear to Cheltenham?" I asked her one morning as I shared some hot chocolate after riding out. It was a dressy race meeting, and I couldn't see even Sue turning up in wellingtons and an old hat, like Paddington Bear.

"Wear?" she answered, as if it was incredibly unusual to wear clothes at all, never mind something special. "Oh, I expect I'll wear my old camel coat."

"One hump or two?" said Ben. "It looks like it's up to you, Becky, to provide our party with its glamour."

Fat chance of that, I thought. Ned had a generous nature, but I knew money was thin on the ground, and it was so long since he'd bought any clothes for himself, that he still thought I could buy a dress for the price of a couple of pairs of tights. I couldn't imagine Jamie Howland being impressed by my 'best' suit, bought for a wedding a year ago. It was blue and made me look, I thought, like a Girl Guide who hadn't won any badges.

But luck and timing were on my side. The very next day, when I got home from school, there was a large parcel for me on the kitchen table. It was covered with American stamps and the customs label on the back declared it was women's clothes and gave their value at an astronomical amount, even allowing for the exchange rate.

"Who can have sent me this?" I said.

Ned looked sheepish, and busied himself with filling Shelley's water bowl. "It's from an old friend of mine – Claudia, who lives in Vero Beach in Florida. I had a letter last month, saying she's coming over for a visit in autumn – or 'the fall' as she puts it. I wrote back, saying she'd be very welcome – and I just mentioned you were becoming quite grown up. I think that," and he gestured at the parcel, "is quite unnecessary and if the price on that label is right, the sun has obviously affected her brain..."

I didn't wait to hear any more, but grabbed the parcel and rushed off to my room. I prayed it wouldn't contain a middle-aged, expensive outfit. It seemed a shame to tear off the amazing gift wrapping – layers of bright tissue paper and reels of satin ribbon. But at last I pulled free a lovely, cream dress and a matching cream jacket, cut a bit like a man's dinner jacket, with long, narrow lapels. I looked at the label– Ralph Lauren.

There was a card with it:

Becky,

I'm such an old friend of Ned's – we go way back to when he played polo over here – that I feel I know you, too.

*I've promised myself that British trip this
year before I get too decrepit, darling!*

*Thought you might have some use for
this – you could wear the jacket with jeans
and a T-shirt – or give it to a thrift shop if
it's not your style.*

Affectionately,

Claudia.

I tore off my old jeans and sweater and
stepped into the dress. My legs were suddenly long and slim, like a colt's, and my hair,
which I always think of as boringly red, tumbled against the expensive cream material like
auburn silk. The dress was cut in such an
amazing way that you didn't even notice it –
only me. I just looked very chic and grown-
up and as if I dressed like that all the time.

As far as I was concerned now, the Sun
Alliance couldn't come soon enough.

"Jamie Howland," I said, twisting round
to see what I looked like from the back, "you
haven't seen anything yet..."

"Wow!" said Ben on the morning of the race

when I strode into the kitchen in my new cream outfit. "Where's Becky then?"

"Search me, Tubby," I replied, tossing my hair and grinning at him.

"What a five-star, thoroughbred outfit," said the Governor, picking some wisps of straw off her camel coat. "I've not seen anything like that in any of my catalogues."

She hated shopping so much, she only ever bought things from catalogues, going for things that were loose and comfortable and didn't show the dirt.

"Even I can tell that didn't come out of a catalogue," said Ben. "I'm only worried that Red Rag won't recognise you – I'm trying to keep him to his routine as much as possible."

I rushed off to see him. "All right, Monkey?" I said. "Now don't get carried away by the atmosphere. Just imagine it's you and me, up the gallops, and let yourself go. I'll be watching."

He nipped at the air beside my ear and I added, "Now, now, don't do that to Jamie Howland – he's very particular who bites his ears, I've heard."

Red Rag emerged from the horsebox at Cheltenham fresh as a daisy. We put him in one of the stables, where he would wait until the race before ours, when we'd take him to the special saddling-up area.

Jamie Howland would still be in the changing room, probably catching some of the races on TV, and dodging the plates of sandwiches and mugs of tea that were always floating about, but which few of the jockeys could eat.

The saddling-up area is like a row of open loose boxes. John, Ben and I saddled up Red Rag and put his new rug over his quarters. Then John took him off to the pre-parade ring, and finally the parade ring, where the owners and punters study all the horses to check their form.

When Ben gave Red Rag a final pat before John led him off, I could see that his hand was a bit shaky. I always think of Ben as a kind of rock – sturdy and reliable – and I was amazed to see that the atmosphere was getting to him. I suppose Cheltenham is to racing what Wimbledon is to tennis – you just can't help feeling the aftershock of past, thrilling events hanging in the air.

I chattered too much as usual as Ben and I walked to the parade ring to wait for Jamie. It was supposed to take Ben's mind off the tension of the wait, but don't ask me what I said.

I was interrupted in mid flow by Jamie coming up to us, looking almost edible in Ben's racing colours of blue and grey silk. Although he'd test driven Red Rag a good few times, I still felt I should tell him how I would tackle the race, because I felt I knew Red Rag better than anyone.

"Sorry, say that again," said Jamie when I was describing how Red Rag jumped the fences. I realised then that he was looking at me in a new way. You didn't have to be psychic to know that he approved of the change in my appearance. He was looking at me as if he'd never seen me before. And he really seemed to be taking in what I was telling him.

Time seemed to speed up then and Ben and I went off to join Sue and Ned. The horses were pulled in to the centre of the parade ring and their quarter sheets taken off. Ben gave Jamie a leg-up on to Red Rag and tightened his girths. John led them round a couple more times and then the lead reins were off and they all cantered down to show the horses the first fence.

It's all part of the ritual. Years ago, jockeys were allowed to jump the first fence as a practice and although that's stopped, they still ride down just to look at it. The excitement was building up all the time and Ben was beginning to look like a human pressure cooker with steam practically coming out of his ears.

He was better once they were off. Jamie set off in the pack and they thundered down the track, with a bit of barging and swearing as the jockeys, well, jockeyed for position. I could see that Jamie was a bit anxious as they approached the first fence – this was very different from Ben's schooling fences – but Red Rag looked as if he was enjoying himself; his ears were going in all directions – and he timed his strides perfectly.

"That's it, Monkey," I breathed. I knew

that Red Rag liked to be up with the front
runners and Jamie said later he'd felt the only
thing to do was go along with it – the horse
had hit his natural rhythm – so he just rested
his hands and let Red Rag hang in there.

This was much more of a real test than all
his novice chases – he could easily have been
outclassed – but he didn't make a single mis-
take over the fences. As they raced down the
final straight, Ben croaked, "He's going to be
placed."

"I should hope so!" said Ned. "I wasn't
planning on contributing to the bookies'
benevolent fund."

Red Rag came third. It was the most
amazing achievement to come third at
Cheltenham in his second-ever race, and
everyone told us so, as if we couldn't work it
out for ourselves. I could see them looking at
our horse – and us – with new eyes.

I ran down with Ben, and when Jamie and
Red Rag came off the course, I'm afraid I
grabbed the reins and I made a bit of a fool of
myself by getting tearful and patting Jamie on
his thigh, as if he was part of Red Rag. I'd

never really understood the expression 'bursting with pride' before, but Ben looked as if he was in danger of doing just that – he was all pink and puffed up. So many people slapped him on the back and said, "Well done," that you'd have thought he'd run the race himself.

We got back to the winners' enclosure and Ben put Red Rag very proudly in front of the third position, while Ned, John and the Governor joined us and we all hugged one another.

"That horse has got a great future," said Jamie.

"Well I hope you'll ride him again," said Ben.

"Just try and stop me," replied Jamie, smiling at me with his wide, lazy smile which made a shiver of excitement run up my spine. That day, we all felt we were in at the beginning of something special.

Only down-to-earth John said, ominously, like the bad fairy at Cinderella's christening, "Red Rag's being noticed now. I bet not everyone wishes him well."

Rubbish, I thought. Things could only get better and better. But life's never quite like that, is it?

CHAPTER FIVE

I was trying to put in some real work towards my GCSEs now.

As far as I could see, they were just a huge nuisance. I knew I wanted to be a trainer, and that was that. If there had been a GCSE in schooling, or jumping, or breeding, I might have been interested.

Ned had hidden my Walkman. I told him I worked better listening to music but he didn't believe me and we had a real row, which ended with me shouting, "Just because in your day it was all slates and chalk!" and rushing out and banging the door.

I was sitting glumly at the kitchen table with my maths books one day, when Ned said, "Just think – maths may come in handy one day. You may want to calculate your winnings."

"Oh, very subtle," I said. "Shouldn't you be making some pastry, or something?"

We both looked at each other and then giggled. In among all the ghastly lists of French vocabulary and dates of battles, I still managed to keep up with the racing gossip. Red Rag was entered for the Whitbread Gold Cup at Sandown, to be ridden by Jamie. We were on first name terms now and he sometimes asked my advice when he was over riding out Red Rag. Jamie also rode for James Mead, a trainer who lived quite near Ben and Sue, but when he rode out there he nearly always stopped off at Ben's on the way home.

"Mead doesn't go in for socialising much," Jamie said one evening as he sprawled on a bench in Sue's kitchen, a glass of Guinness in one hand and a lump of fruit cake in the other. "And his fruit cake's not as good."

"It's not fair," said Sue, "wait till you're forty-something and you only have to look at a raisin to put on weight."

"We all know the Whitbread Gold Cup is weighted," added Ben. "But Jamie has never had any problems in that respect."

I looked over from my corner where I'd been polishing some tack. Jamie's jaw, as he chewed the fruit cake, was taut as a tightened girth. Jamie had a naturally athletic body. I felt myself blushing, so I bent over the tack and polished extra hard.

"Just think – Red Rag's first handicap chase," said Sue.

"Mead's got a horse in it, too," said Jamie. "Hissing Sid – and try saying that after a glass of Guinness. He's got high hopes for him. He tells me that horse is going to make his fortune."

"I'm surprised he tells you anything," said Sue. "He certainly keeps himself to himself. I felt really sorry for him when his wife ran off with that French trainer, leaving him all alone with the young lad. I asked him over to supper a few times, but he was always too busy. But the son must be about your age now, Jamie."

I wasn't saying anything. Mead's son,

Adam, a jockey, had been the first boy to ask me out. Correction. He is the only boy ever to have asked me out. Unfortunately, he's so wet you could wring him out and has had what Chrissie calls a personality by-pass. But I'd had my eye on Hissing Sid and I'd kept up with his form in the *Racing Post*, and I knew that he was a serious rival for Red Rag.

I'd seen Adam, hanging around watching Jamie schooling Red Rag. He watched them really intently – probably hoping to pick up some tips, I thought. His father wouldn't let him ride Hissing Sid. Adam had ridden in lots of races, and was making quite a name for himself, but his own father didn't think he was up to much, and didn't mind telling him so – and anyone else who wanted to stay round the grumpy old chap long enough to listen.

It was a perfect spring evening – one of those flukes that are more like summer, but newly minted, with no midges hanging round the stables yet.

"Let's hitch Brian up to the cart and take a picnic into the country," said Ben.

For some reason, Jamie didn't have to dash off on some high-powered date, and we were all in the same mood. Sue produced a huge wedge of Cheddar, home-made rolls, apples and cider, and we trotted and cantered along the lanes between the cow parsley. We sat in a field to have our picnic.

"This must be a bit of a come-down for you," I said, as Jamie tossed his hair out of his eyes and took a swig of cider. "I bet you're used to lobster and Champagne."

"Well that just shows how little you know me," he said. "And I'm surprised you have time to read the gossip columns – aren't you meant to be doing your homework?"

I could have hit him but then he went on, "Actually, my favourite food is a meat pie and some hot Bovril – on the terraces."

"At a football match?" I said.

"Well, yes – good restaurants tend not to have terraces," he said.

"But I love football!" I said, forgetting to be angry.

He flashed his amazing blue eyes at me and when he saw I was serious, he said,

"Would you like to come along to a match some time?"

Watching a football match with Jamie Howland. Sharing a pie and Bovril. There is a God! I thought.

"I might," I said, "if I've got no home-work."

On our way home, we passed James Mead on a large black horse. They both looked rather sullen, and when we called out a cheery greeting, Mead only grunted and touched his hat so briefly you would have thought it was poisoned.

"He must be lonely," said Ben, "but it's as if he doesn't want to be friends."

He looked after the hunched, disappearing figure and added, "It's as if he wants quite the reverse."

I wore what I thought of as my 'lucky' outfit – Claudia's wonderful present – to Sandown for the Whitbread Gold Cup. We pulled up quite near to what I recognised as the Meads'

horsebox, and Adam appeared from round the back, wearing the most revolting pair of mustard-coloured cords, tight in all the wrong places.

"Hi, Becky," he said. "Do you fancy getting together later?"

I'd already refused his offer of a date once and this only confirmed that he had the sensitivity of a bathmat.

"Sorry, Adam," I said, "I'm doing something later." Of course I had nothing planned, but secretly I hoped I would be sharing a celebration with Jamie.

Then Mead appeared. "You haven't got time to lounge about chatting," he snapped at Adam. "It's time Sid was saddled up. I don't want anything to go wrong at this stage. He's a cert to win," he shouted over his shoulder at me as he left.

We'll see about that, I thought.

But in fact Hissing Sid did come in first – only half a length in front of Red Rag.

"It's brilliant to come second in his first handicapped race," said Ben and we all agreed. But I could see he was annoyed that he'd been beaten by a horse of Mead's. But Ben is the perfect sportsman, and, when we were all gathered in the winners' enclosure – "I'm getting quite used to this," I said to Sue – he strode over and put out his huge, work-worn hand to Mead.

But Mead only gave it the briefest of shakes, said, "Right, thanks," and turned on his heel and marched away. I knew that train-ers are the most competitive beings on the planet, but this was going a bit far. Ben looked totally nonplussed and then I could see him getting angry.

"Right," he said. "We'll show him. If that's the way he wants to play it."

Jamie was travelling back with us, so we waited while he changed and had a quick drink with some of the jockeys and other trainers.

"The talk is that Mead has totally flipped his lid," he said when he joined us. "He's say-ing that Hissing Sid is going to sweep the board next season. And he had large bets on Sid to win." Ben nearly crashed into a verge when he added, "He's saying Red Rag should be renamed Limp Rag. Adam kept trying to butt in and say Sid's success was all down to him – you know how Adam wants to be a trainer. But his father completely ignored him and talked through him.

"'You're like a wet weekend. What would *you* know about training horses?' he asked Adam, very loudly, in the middle of the crowded bar."

Poor Adam. No wonder he was desperate to make some money and leave home as soon as possible. He hadn't the life of a dog. I felt so sorry for him that I almost wished I had agreed to go out with him and cheer him up.

But then I caught sight of Jamie's reflection in the wing mirror, where I could study him without being seen. He was fresh from his shower, and his dark hair was wet and brushed back, making him as appealing as a baby seal. If you want something badly enough, I thought, that's half the battle. Ben now desperately wants Red Rag to beat Hissing Sid. And me? Well, that would be telling.

CHAPTER SIX

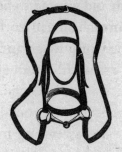

"Why are we having so much fish?" I asked
Ned, as I helped myself to a second smoked
haddock fishcake.

"Everyone knows it's good for the brain,"
said Ned, plopping a huge dollop of parsley
sauce on to his plate.

Of course, I should have known. My
English GCSE was the next day. I had spent
hours in my bedroom making revision
timetables. If I'd spent as much time actually
revising, I wouldn't have this heavy feeling in
my stomach now.

I phoned Chrissie to see how she was
feeling. "There's nothing you can actually do
at this stage," she said. "You've either got it
or you haven't."

I sort of felt I hadn't. Chrissie was brilliant at English and wanted to be a journalist. She ran up a fortune on her mother's newspaper bill buying every magazine in sight and saying it was 'research'. I thought she would go far.

Sue and Ben sent me a good luck card and I lost a whole day's revising because Jamie dropped off an old horseshoe for luck and I found it impossible to think about French verbs afterwards. It was a relief when the GCSEs actually started. Our form teacher said we should get some fresh air between exams, and I took him at his word, rushing over to see Red Rag whenever I could.

"Lucky old Monkey," I said to him. "You don't need to sit any exams – all you have to do is reach your potential."

I told myself that I didn't care about the results but when the fateful day arrived, it was torture driving over to the school with Ned to pick up the brown envelope.

"It's barbaric," said Ned. "In my day, they arrived through the letter box."

I could hardly read the pieces of paper

inside, as all around me friends shrieked with joy or wept with despair. Chrissie had got a starred A in English and was carrying on as if she'd won the Nobel prize for literature.

But in the end I did all right – one A, in Maths, which would come in handy if I wanted to become a bookie, three Bs and three Cs, which Ned seemed to think was enough to merit opening one of his few remaining, dusty bottles of Bollinger.

As the pale biscuit-coloured bubbles tickled the back of my throat, I toasted my own future.

I was sixteen now and Ned agreed that I could leave school and work in the Mainwaring's yard. Ben had drawn up a contract, making me Assistant Trainer – which sounded very grand – but in fact meant I would be paid agricultural wages and would be glad of Ned's cooking for a long time to come.

What had finally swung it with Ned, was

talking to some of the parents at an end of year wine and cheese party. Lots of them had enthused about their children having work experience.

"It makes them much more mature. And often, the real world of work makes studying seem much more attractive. Gregory is working with orang-utans in Borneo, and then he'll do his A levels at the college..."

I think Ned thought that after a couple of months eating, drinking and sleeping horses, I would be glad to get back to a nice warm classroom. How wrong could he be?

But I'm jumping on a bit. After I'd sat my GCSEs and was waiting for my results, there was a lull and the summer stretched ahead. I had no more studying and the Mainwarings were coping well on their own. They were expecting a couple of new horses to be placed with them, but not for a few weeks.

Word of Red Rag's performance at Cheltenham and Sandown had spread as fast as these things do in racing circles. It's a very gossipy world and I'd grown to love this aspect of it. So, for the first time for ages, I had time on my hands.

So it seemed fated when Jamie said one day, "Mead's having trouble with staff."

"So, what's new?" asked Sue, as the three of us trotted down the lane towards the farm.

"He needs someone to help ride out – just for a couple of weeks," went on Jamie. "I just thought of Becky – as you're a bit slack just at the minute. The only thing is, it would mean staying in Mead's hostel, but I'm often over there and I could keep an eye on her."

The idea of Jamie keeping an eye on me almost made me break into a gallop but I managed to appear quite calm.

"I think that's a good idea," I said. "I could earn a bit of extra money – and my contract with you and Ben doesn't start, officially, till the new season."

I talked it over with Ned that night.

"You've never stayed away from home before," he said. "You'll probably live on cornflakes and those horrible things called Noodle Pots that I've seen on television."

"It would be good for me," I said. "I can't go through life cossetted and fed on gourmet food like some pampered pussy cat."

Ned looked quite hurt, so I went over and gave him a quick kiss on the top of his head, where his hair's beginning to thin. The truth was, I didn't know if it would be good for me or not. Perhaps I would be terribly homesick. Or perhaps Ned would think it wasn't worth cooking for one and start living on fish fingers and spaghetti hoops.

If I worked at Mead's, I wouldn't see Red Rag and no one else could communicate with him as well as I could – not even Jamie. But I had to think of my career. So I wrote to Mead, putting down my experience at the Mainwarings, although I was sure Jamie would have mentioned me to him.

Two days later, Mead rang up when I was out and barked at Ned: "Tell Rebecca tomorrow, 10 am, in the yard," and then hung up.

"Where was he when they were handing out charm?" asked Ned, when I came in.

I smiled. "Chrissie says Mead thinks charisma is the 25th of December..."

But I was very serious and professional when I met Mead in his yard. I always think

Mead's yard looks a bit sad, like a supermodel who's gone to seed and slops about in an old tracksuit. It used to belong to a really ace trainer, about ten years ago, and there's stabling for ninety boxes and a lovely big house. But it's all a bit run down now and in need of a good lick of paint. The garden's wild; the hedges round Mead's house are real Sleeping Beauty stuff.

"I thought you were tied up with the Mainwarings and their bionic wonder horse," said Mead.

"I am," I explained, "but it just happens to be a slack time just now – before the new horses arrive. The yard's reputation is spreading," I couldn't help adding, loyally.

"That's just beginner's luck," said Mead. "However, it's hard to get short-term staff, and beggars can't be choosers."

I waited, but that seemed to be it. I gathered I'd got the job and then Adam appeared and said he would show me the hostel where I was to stay, with the other girls.

"I expect we'll be seeing a lot more of each other now," he said. He could do with seeing a lot more of a hot flannel and a decent haircut, but I didn't say so.

I shared the hostel with three girls. We all loved horses, of course, and we had brilliant times, lying on our beds talking about how we would be famous trainers.

"And when I win the National," said Sophie, who was blonde with large green eyes and obsessed with clothes, "I see myself in the winners' enclosure in a very pale pink Catherine Walker."

"What the hell's a Catherine Walker?" shrieked Jessie, who was dark and plump and lived in jodhpurs, and Fay, who was fey as well as Fay and mousey all over, added, "Wouldn't you be better in a dress?"

We had a phone but it only took incoming calls, because Mead didn't trust us not to run up huge bills. But nearly all the calls were for Sophie, from the male species. She seemed to spend more time rubbing in hand cream than she did mucking out. In fact, when there was a boring or dirty job, she seemed to be invisible.

One day Sophie looked out of the window and saw Adam pottering about the yard. "He really gives me the creeps," she said. "He looks as if he needs worming."

Adam had asked them all out, one after the other, so not only was he the only boy who'd ever asked me out, he was totally indiscriminate.

Oh well, there were always the horses. The yard was quite well run – it was much bigger than the Mainwarings' and had a quarantine yard round the back, which was strictly out-of-bounds. Mead made a real song and dance about us staying away from it.

"What has he got round there?" drawled Sophie. "Cholera?"

"Or Adam – 'the beast that came from the hay loft,'" said Jessie.

Jamie came over quite a few times, to help get the horses fit for the next season.

"Hi there Pusscat," he shouted at me the first time he came.

"*What* did you call me!" I exclaimed.

"Pusscat – because when you're angry, Becky, you're just like a cat flicking its tail." He grinned, tossing his hair back.

"Do you practise that in a mirror?" I shouted back.

"You don't mean you actually *know* that Greek god?" said Sophie later. "Not *the* Jamie Howland?" I had seen her out of the corner of my eye, in the yard, watching while Jamie and I laughed and teased each other, her mouth hanging open, wide enough to attract several horse flies.

"Jamie?" I replied, casually. "He's just a very good friend. Worse luck, I added to myself, under my breath.

In fact Jamie and I rode out together a few times. It was wonderful to ride with him and I think that countryside and that time of year will always be my idea of heaven. And Jamie telling me about Red Rag was the next best thing to riding him myself.

Living in the hostel was very different from life with Ned. Well, Ned never put a dead mouse in my riding boot – but one of Mead's lads did. And when it was Jessie's birthday, all her presents were hidden in a huge pile of freshly mucked-out straw, still warm and pungent, like a gigantic, smelly lucky dip. Of course, it didn't bother Jessie in the slightest – she went straight in like a ferret and pulled them out.

Sophie looked on in horror and drawled, "Isn't that a bit *infantile?*" as if she was a hundred-and-fifty.

Then one of the lads decided to have a fancy-dress party. 'Your ultimate dream' was the theme. Jessie spent every spare moment making herself a huge, cream bun outfit from net and cotton wool. Sophie pinned *Vogue* covers all over a simple, dangerously short black dress.

"Why doesn't she just take along a mirror?" grumbled Fay. She couldn't get into the bathroom because Sophie was waxing her legs. Every now and again there was a loud shriek from behind the closed door, as if Sophie was being slowly and painfully murdered.

Fay looked very dashing in a suit and bow tie. Everyone had to ask what she was and she said she was a very rich bookie – she was fed up with being poor.

It was no secret that my dream was to be a

top trainer. I tried on a stretchy black body, a short lycra skirt and fishnet tights.

"I didn't know your ultimate dream was to be a tart, Becky," said Sophie when she saw me. "That shouldn't be too difficult."

But I wasn't finished. I got lots of old rosettes that were pinned up in the tack room and I stitched them all over the body and skirt, keeping two large blue ones for the front. The effect was amazing. Even Sophie was struck dumb for once and when we arrived at the party I could see Jamie, out of the corner of my eye, doing a double take.

Sophie rushed over to him and admired his outfit – he was looking unbelievable in striped silk pyjamas; he said he lived at such a fast pace that his ultimate dream was a week in bed. It was a good line and I could see Sophie practically fainting when he flashed her one of his looks.

She really monopolised him, hanging on his every word and telling him what a brilliant jockey he was. In the end, I got fed up and went home early. I could feel Jamie's eyes following me out, boring even more holes into my fishnet tights.

About three days after the party, the phone rang at the hostel. Jessie answered and I heard her say, "No – she's not here just now. Righto."

"For Sophie?" I asked when she came back.

"Yes – it was that jockey, you know, Jamie Howland."

My stomach lurched and I pushed away my dinner. I didn't think I would feel like eating ever again.

I kept telling myself that I'd been really stupid to think that Jamie thought of me as anything more or less than a friend. A pal. A chum. About as attractive as a bowl of dog food. I'd thought Jamie was not just another superficial guy, heavily into ego massage by the nearest pretty face.

I was relieved when my three weeks were up. Four new horses had arrived at the

Mainwarings and they needed every pair of hands they could find. Flytrap and Red Rag were both being schooled towards national hunt races and Red Rag was being fine tuned for his first season.

"You seem a bit off colour since you came home," said Ned one evening. "It's probably all that hostel food."

"You make it sound like a prison," I said, "but the other girls were really friendly. I had a great time," I added, glumly.

"So I can see. Why don't you ask them over one evening? I'll make a jug of Pimms."

I didn't want Ned to think I was turning into a recluse, so I agreed, on condition that he let me buy in some pizzas.

"Well, all right," he said, "though why we've all got to pretend we're Neapolitan workers, I don't know. You're not asking that Jamie Howland, are you?" added Ned.

"Of course not," I said sharply. "Why on earth would I?"

"I just thought – at one time – you were seeing rather a lot of him," said Ned. "I saw something about him in the local paper.

There was a picture of him with a girl on each arm. In my view, he's mad, bad and dangerous to know."

"I couldn't agree more," I said, turning on my heel.

Jessie and Fay jumped from the Range Rover Fay had driven over, and gave me huge hugs. Sophie, perfectly and icily clad from head to foot in pale blue, was already charming Ned.

"I'd love to hear about when you played polo," she said, "it always sounds so thrilling."

Then she turned to me. "It's good to see you – and how's your friend, the glamorous Jamie Howland? I must say, we've not seen nearly so much of him since you left."

"My friend?" I asked stupidly. "I thought he'd become your friend. I remember him ringing you at the hostel," I added bitterly.

Sophie's green eyes grew even bigger. "You mean, you and Jamie aren't, you know, but I thought, well I assumed really... But never mind. That's fascinating."

"Wait a minute," said Jessie to me. "I think I can fill in here. That time Jamie rang up for Sophie, it was just to tell her to put on the extra lightweight saddle in the next schooling session.

"Yes – it was a really silly message, I'd forgotten all about it," said Sophie, blushing.

Just like you've forgotten about desperately trying to get off with him at the party, I thought.

"Of all the jockeys I've worked with," said Jessie, "Jamie Howland is the best at dealing with horses – he knows their needs before they do."

I suddenly felt that the new season was going to be a fresh beginning on all sorts of fronts.

CHAPTER SEVEN

The 'fall' arrived and, shortly afterwards, Ned's old friend, Claudia, from Florida. I was expecting someone in the autumn of her years, treating herself to a restful holiday in a country cottage. But Claudia was slim and tall, with a light tan and blonde streaks and descended on Ned like a whirlwind.

"It's *so* wonderful to see you," she shouted, when the taxi driver had emptied five cases out of his boot and driven away, beaming, and wildly overtipped. "And just look at this darling cottage – it's like something out of Disneyworld."

"No dwarfs inside, but authentic cobwebs if you look hard enough," I gabbled, out of nerves.

"Becky!" she screeched, as if I were her long-lost child. "We're going to have such fun. You must take me shopping. I haven't brought a thing with me."

Ned looked pointedly at the cases piled up beside her and said, "Would you like to lie down? Jet lag and all that..."

"All in the mind," said Claudia briskly. "I took some homoeopathic drops and I'm wearing one of my healing crystals on a chain."

"Well, come in and have some tea," said Ned, "but I can't promise it'll be homoeo-whatsit."

"I want *English* tea," said Claudia, flinging out her arms on the way into the cottage, as if she was going to embrace the lintels.

I was quite glad next morning that I had a job to go to, because Claudia's enthusiasm for everything – the house, the food, the countryside – was exhausting.

My work at the Mainwarings had started in earnest, because the new season was looming and Red Rag was entered for the Tetley Chase at Wetherby in October and the

Hennessy in November. This was one more step towards the Gold Cup in March and it was important to keep him on top form.

The Mainwarings had four new horses now and as well as schooling them and riding out, it was important to keep the two owners happy. I learnt how to make egg-and-cress sandwiches and Earl Grey tea and talk about their horses in the best possible light, stressing their potential. But none of them measured up to Red Rag.

"I missed you, silly old Monkey," I told him. "And I can tell you missed me."

His ears moved in that unique way they had, telegraphing his affection for me.

I think I bored Claudia so much, telling her about Red Rag, that finally she had to ask to see him. Or 'meet him' as she put it. When I took her over to the yard, Jamie was just getting back from schooling him.

"Why, he's darling!" Claudia exclaimed. I looked at her and she was staring straight into Jamie's eyes – he might as well have been riding a cart horse. "Mmm," she said, "a really neat package."

"He's got amazing hindquarters," I said wickedly. "Talk about stamina!"

For a moment, Claudia looked quite taken aback, then she laughed and agreed. "Oh yes – the horse, he's simply divine."

I introduced Jamie to Claudia. At once, they both turned on batteries of charm and I found it a bit overwhelming, so I went off to find Sue and organise some tea.

When Claudia was out one day, frightening the village hairdresser with requests for head massages and root-lifting mousses, Ned sat down wearily with a cup of coffee and suggested we have a dinner party.

"You mean spread the load?" I laughed.

"Well, it would be good for Claudia to meet some other people."

I saw how I could kill several birds with one stone and asked Ben and Sue and the two new owners.

The owners were as different as chalk and cheese. David's family had bred horses for generations. He'd watched Red Rag's progress with interest, and then decided to stable two of his horses with Ben.

The nearest Victor had come to racing, however, was watching it on television. Until, that is, the red letter day when he won the lottery. The Governor called him Mr X behind his back: "He certainly didn't put an X for no publicity, did he?" she said after the first time she met him.

Victor had first arrived at the yard with his horses, wearing a sheepskin coat that was so new it creaked when he moved his arms. On one of his arms was his wife, Wendy, dressed more for a garden party than a tour of a muddy yard.

"We'd love to come to dinner," said Victor when I asked them. "I expect we could pick up some good tips, too."

"Like buying some wellies," said the Governor under her breath.

"I'm going to do the cooking," I told Ned the day before the dinner party. "I'm sure entertaining owners is part of my contract. You take Claudia down to the pub, *The*

White Horse, tomorrow for a drink, and don't come back until about eight."

Claudia had fallen in love with our very ordinary, slightly run-down pub, and Ned had weaned her off cocktails on to halves of bitter. She lived in hope that someone would have a game of shove ha'penny with her and didn't believe Ned when he said people preferred playing the one-armed bandit.

When I was out buying the food, I ran into Adam Mead in our small supermarket.

"How's Red Rag?" he asked.

I was always so happy to talk about my favourite horse, that I launched into some technical chit-chat and quite forgot I was speaking to the grisly Adam.

"D'you want to have a coffee and a chat?" asked Adam, scratching a spot on his neck.

He suddenly seemed very interested in Red Rag, but I said, "No thanks. And it'll never get well if you pick it," pointing to his neck and rushed off to the safety of the frozen food cabinet.

The dinner party turned out to be friendly and old-fashioned and just up Claudia's street. She kept going on about how typically British it was and even found Ned's jokey horse-riding table mats funny. I didn't have the heart to tell her that most people I knew ate off trays in front of the TV.

She and Wendy were getting on like a house on fire and I could hear them planning a shopping trip. Claudia tried to persuade the Governor to go with them, but she looked at Claudia as if she was mad.

"You mean you go shopping for fun?"

"That's right," said Claudia gaily. "Shop till you drop."

"I just throw the Governor the odd horse blanket at Christmas and such like," said Ben, "and they usually suit her a treat."

Claudia looked shocked for a moment, until she realised it was British, straight-faced humour. The whole table dissolved in laughter – and I don't think she realised we were all laughing at her expression.

"I like the sound of your yard," I heard her saying to Ben at the coffee and brandy stage. "If Ned can find me a horse that's a good buy – I trust his judgement absolutely – could I put him in training with you?"

"It looks as if our business is booming by the minute," said Ben.

I'm afraid brandy tastes like cough medicine to me, so after dinner I sat beside the fire nursing a glass of red wine. The future looked just as rosy, so why did I feel slightly uneasy? And why was Adam Mead suddenly so interested in Red Rag?

CHAPTER EIGHT

Jamie came over about once every two weeks to ride out Red Rag, just to keep the feel of him. Sometimes he complimented me on my riding – my rapport with Red Rag – and I thought, I bet all these blonde bimbos who are after him can't take a jump like that. I bet Sophie would be too worried about her mascara running. For the moment, I was content with riding out with him and catching up on the gossip he always brought with him.

On the days when I was meeting the owners, I took extra care to dress a bit more smartly than usual. Claudia had taken me and Chrissie on one of her famous shopping trips and insisted on buying me a man's huge, pale pink, cashmere sweater, which I threw on over my jodhpurs when I hoped Jamie might be dropping in.

"It's the least I can do, for all your hospitality," she said.

Chrissie had wanted to hear all about New York. "I plan to go there and write about it some day," she said.

Claudia frog-marched her into a bookshop and bought her a fat book of black and white photographs of New York. On her way to the till she picked up the *New Yorker* and the American *Vanity Fair*. Chrissie just kept repeating, "Thank you, thank you," – very unlike someone with a gift for language.

"Now, let's buy something for poor Sue. How about a silk headscarf – although she'd really be better off with a trip to Vidal Sassoon..."

I managed to persuade her that 'poor Sue' would probably use the scarf to clean the car windscreen.

"If you must buy her a present," I said, "she would love a new set of racing silks."

I was right, Sue was thrilled and Claudia soared in her estimation.

One morning, Sue was happily frying some eggs for a late breakfast, when Jamie appeared.

"Perfect timing, as ever," he grinned. "Make mine crispy round the edges, with some bacon for company."

"Any news?" I asked him, looking up from the *Racing Post*. Ned had given me a subscription for my birthday and I was becoming a walking encyclopedia on form and results.

"Well, Mead is losing more staff," said Jamie. "There's something funny about that yard, but I can't put my finger on it. He's looking for someone to come and help ride out – just for a couple of weeks, until he gets a replacement."

Because Mead found it difficult to get, and keep, staff, he paid quite well. As I had already worked there and knew the ropes, I persuaded Ben to let me go over there for two weeks. Red Rag had already run well at the Tetley and Hennessy being placed second and third, and was having a couple of easy weeks. I would be back in plenty of time to get him ready for the King George V at Kempton on Boxing Day.

"I'll be back weeks before that," I assured him. "I can't leave Ned in Claudia's clutches all over Christmas – she'll make him wear a long red hat with a bobble on the end and cover the cottage in plastic snow."

I was packing for Mead's yard when the phone rang.

"It's that cute jockey," Claudia yelled upstairs.

"Becky – it's Jamie," said a deep, Marmitey voice. "I've got an extra ticket for the match on Saturday and wondered if you'd be interested. Racing has been cancelled because of last week's freeze, but luckily the football's still on."

"Saturday," I repeated, "I think that's fine..."

Claudia was grinning and giving me the thumbs up. The first thing she said when I put the phone down was, "Now, what are you going to wear? What is it he's asked you to – is it an intimate dinner, or one of those fabulous English balls?"

"It's a football match," I said, which threw her a bit, but not for long.

"I see. We're talking spectator clothing," she said. "What about a beige cashmere duffel coat?"

When Saturday came, there was a biting wind and I wore my familiar, comfortable leather jacket. I did spend a long time, however, washing and blowdrying my hair and applying make-up in such a subtle way that it looked as if I wasn't wearing any.

Jamie picked me up in his MG, which of course Claudia thought was 'just adorable', and as we sped off, I looked forward to some time on our own – a chance to get to know him over a hot pie and a mug of Bovril.

Fat chance! We arrived at the ground and Jamie jumped out of the car and said, "We're meeting the others inside."

Inside the gates, we were greeted by five of Jamie's jockey friends and most of the girls from Mead's yard.

Oh well! At least it was a good game and it was good to see Jessie there, jumping up and down, cheering on both sides.

When I went back to Mead's yard to work, I wasn't surprised to find that Sophie had gone – apparently to Lord Somebody's stud in Gloucestershire. She would probably end up marrying his dashing son and never carry another shovelful of manure in her life, I thought, as I mucked out Hissing Sid's stable.

But Fay and Jessie were pleased to see me.

"Mead's getting worse," said Fay. "I don't think he'll hang on to any of his owners if he keeps barking down the phone at them. He's obsessed with Hissing Sid and he couldn't care less about the other horses."

"And he's even more paranoid about the quarantine yard," went on Jessie. "There was a programme on the telly the other day about stress and they told you symptoms to look out for. Apparently I'm as stressed as a wet loofah, but Mead is heading for a breakdown. And Adam doesn't seem to care – he's always dashing off on business of his own."

"Probably to the chemist to stock up on cream for boils and piles," I said.

I couldn't help thinking about the quarantine yard. I don't know why somewhere out of bounds becomes so attractive, but finally I could resist it no longer. I waited until one evening when no one was about and sneaked round to the yard.

No bodies. No half-starved horse tied up in the corner. Not even Adam, waiting to pounce and convince me that he was Tom Cruise in disguise. (Some disguise.)

All I found were two horses, standing there quite relaxed and happy. I thought perhaps there was some bug going round. Mead wouldn't want people to know there was a bug in the yard, so he'd put these two horses in quarantine until they were safe. Very sensible behaviour for someone teetering on the brink of a nervous breakdown. Reassured, I crept back to the hostel.

But a few nights later I was lying in my bed. It was only half-past ten but I was really tired, having worked flat out all day – so much so, that I was just thinking I could see why Mead had wanted me back, even if I did work for a rival trainer. I was just drifting off to sleep, when I heard what sounded like a football match. I rubbed my eyes, but I wasn't dreaming.

Anyway, when I heard this football match, I thought it must be Mead, watching television. I was about to lie down again, when I heard another noise that made me sit up in bed, suddenly not tired at all.

It was the noise of a horse kicking. I immediately thought one of the horses might have got cast – rolled over in its stall and got its legs stuck against the wall. I knew from Ben that there was a danger of a cast horse wrenching its gut, or even breaking a leg, so I threw on my jeans and a sweatshirt and ran outside, following the noise.

It was coming from quite far away and as I got nearer it was clear it was coming from the quarantine yard. I could hear a horse panicking, as well as a football crowd cheering, but the strange thing was that both noises were coming from the quarantine yard. I ran past Mead's house, and it was in darkness.

I ran as fast as I could and was almost at the yard, when the noise of the football match stopped abruptly. I was aware that the horse had stopped kicking, too.

At the same moment, I could hear footsteps behind me. I wished it wasn't pitch dark away from the house and that I wasn't on my own. Jessie and Fay were at the cinema – I had stayed behind because I was dead on my feet.

Someone coughed and then spat loudly on the ground. That sounded disgusting enough for Adam.

"Is that you, Adam?" I said, trying to make my voice very matter-of-fact.

"It's Mead senior," said Mead, "and I thought I told you to stay away from the quarantine yard. What the Hell are you doing here at this time of night?"

He sounded menacing and he was swishing a crop gently against his side, as if weighing up what to do with it. As he came nearer and my eyes adjusted to the dark, I could see that he was in his dressing gown and slippers. I wished with all my heart that I was back in my bed.

"I heard noises..." I began.

"So did I," said Adam, coming out of the

shadows with a torch, as if he'd just been to the quarantine yard.

"What is this – a cocktail party?" said Mead.

"Adam!" I gasped with relief. I never thought I would be pleased to see him.

"I was just watching the match on television when I heard a horse kicking, so I thought I'd better check it – it's all right now," Adam said. "Becky's just being careful," he went on, "we don't want anything to happen to our horses, do we?"

Mead grunted and seemed to lose interest. "That's twice you've been told to stay away from that yard," he said to me. "It will definitely not be third time lucky for you. But you won't get the chance," he went on. "I want you out of here first thing in the morning. You hear and see too much. I'm not so desperate for workers that I need to put up with the likes of you.

"I'll dare say you were hoping it was my Sid in a bit of trouble – terminal, even. This is a professional yard. Why don't you run on back to the Mainwairing's *amateur* set-up. Quite frankly, they couldn't run a bath, let alone a proper yard!"

I didn't need to be told twice. My two weeks were almost up, anyway, and I was missing Red Rag dreadfully. If Mead had wanted to make us more determined that Red Rag would beat Hissing Sid at Kempton, he couldn't have planned it any better.

"I'll see you back to the hostel," said Adam.

As we walked along he said, "Don't mind Dad – he's under a lot of pressure. He told me himself, in one of his mellower moments, that he thinks you've got a real gift with horses."

Adam sounded almost civilised for once. Of course, the fact that it was dark and I couldn't really see him helped a lot.

But in the morning he came over to say goodbye. In the cold light of day he looked just as bad as ever – in a felted sweater the colour of dung and hair that needed washing.

"I hope you won't hold last night against me," he said.

The idea of holding anything against

Adam made me feel quite ill. I was eager to get back to Ned and Claudia and normality. There was something in the air at Mead's yard. I couldn't put my finger on it, but when you spend all your time working and communicating with horses, after a while you develop a sixth sense. I just knew there was something weird going on. I just felt it in my bones.

CHAPTER NINE

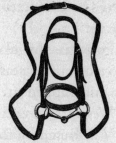

I got home to find that Claudia had transformed the cottage with very upmarket decorations. There wasn't a paper chain or a bit of tinsel in sight, but you couldn't move without bumping into boughs of fir tree with scarlet apples wired on to them.

The Christmas tree had real candles, which Claudia was going to light for just enough time to take photographs before they became a fire hazard. It was kitted out with dried orange slices and cinnamon sticks, and the fairy at the top – which I had made at nursery school out of the inside of a toilet roll and some paper doilys, which Ned always puts on – looked totally embarrassed and out of place.

Christmas morning was as crisp and white

and sparkly as it's meant to be. I went over to the Mainwaring's first thing to ride out with Ben, Sue and John.

"Happy Christmas, Monkey," I said to Red Rag, who telegraphed season's greetings with his ears and nipped at my arm as I stroked him. We were all excited about the King George V at Kempton the next day. It was run at level weights, like the Gold Cup, and we knew it would be a good pointer to how he would run at Cheltenham.

I cycled back to the cottage, where Ned was basting a large goose and Claudia was knocking back Bucks Fizz and rabbiting on about *A Christmas Carol* and the magic of a traditional Christmas, with "real logs on the fire".

"Have a Bucks Fizz, Becky darling," she said to me. "The vitamin C in the orange juice will do you the world of good."

She'd got completely caught up too in the excitement of Red Rag's progress towards the Gold Cup and obviously wasn't dreaming of going home before then.

Sometimes she talked about the old days

in Florida, when Ned had played polo. I could tell she fancied him like mad, but to Ned she would never be anything more than a good friend. Just like me and Jamie.

True to her word, Claudia had dragged Ned round countless studs, looking for a horse. When they came back from these outings, she seemed to be much more clued up on the people than the horses.

"Someone should tell that trainer's wife that she can't wear pastels," she said after one trip.

"But what about the horse, Claudia?" said Ned in despair.

"Well, I guess it can wear whatever it likes." said Claudia, "I'm not really into horse blankets."

I knew she saw buying a horse, more than anything, as a way of keeping in touch.

"I know I'll be in the States and it'll be here, but I can nip over from time to time to see him," she said.

Finally, they found a big, dark brown horse and Claudia bought it for over £20,000. She could afford it because her husband, a lot older than she and now long dead, had been, as she put it, 'in oil', which always made me think of him as a sardine. She stabled it with Ben.

"What's his name?" asked Sue as we all looked him over.

"I want to call him 'Ned's chukka'," said Claudia coyly.

"Don't be so damn silly," said Ned in embarrassment. "How about 'Long Distance'?"

In the end, they decided on Florida's Hopes, and Claudia spent hours in the paddock taking video films of him to show the folks back home.

Christmas was as traditional as Claudia could have wished for, from the carol singers at the pub to the plum pudding and brandy butter. But the whole day was only a prelude for me. I went to bed early, leaving Ned and Claudia in front of a huge fire with their mulled wine. I felt a tight, excited feeling in my stomach – the sort of feeling that's usually kept for Christmas Eve – because the next day Jamie would ride Red Rag at Kempton and they would both have another chance to prove themselves. I knew Jamie would bring out the best in Red Rag.

"Lucky old Red Rag," I said to myself, as I jumped under my duvet.

It felt like a real family outing – Ned, Claudia, Ben, Sue, John and me.

"I want to put some money on Red Rag," said Claudia when we had arrived at Kempton and she had adjusted her new red hat in the wing mirror of the horsebox.

"Aren't Americans awful? So loud!" said Ben, slapping her on the back. He was really pleased that she shared our confidence and he took her over to Jerry Tidmarsh, his best mate among the bookies.

Jamie appeared from the changing room, in his blue and grey silks.

"What a darling outfit!" said Claudia.

Jamie filled me in on the latest changing-room gossip. Mead was putting a huge sum on Hissing Sid to win.

"But we'll see about that," smiled Jamie.

I had taken extra care to dress up a bit and I saw him taking in my camel coat and long black boots. I was grateful for the money I was earning now, because I could buy the odd new outfit for times like this and Ned had started complaining that, between Claudia and me, he could hardly get into the bathroom to shave.

"The thing about this race," went on Jamie, "is that at level weights *the* very best horse wins."

"And the best jockey," I said.

Jamie smiled, reached out and pushed a long strand of hair back from my face, making my stomach turn over. But then he had to dash off to the centre of the parade ring and I watched as Ben gave him a leg-up and had a quick, final word.

"They're off!" screamed Claudia, shortly afterwards, and a few people right in front of us turned and stared.

"We've got a horse running," she said confidingly. "Red Rag – and he's going to win."

As usual, Red Rag set off with the front runners and there was the usual worry that he might not be able to sustain that position all the way round. Half-way through the race, Hissing Sid thundered up from behind and put on a real spurt. I could see Mead, quite near us, purple in the face, with Adam hanging about beside him like a wet weekend, watching much more coldly, as if he was thinking about something else.

Another chestnut horse – Prairie Rose – suddenly appeared, as if from nowhere, and ran neck-and-neck with Hissing Sid, only about half a length behind Red Rag. When the final fence loomed, Red Rag used his natural pacing to glide over it, landing a length in front of the other two – all three far ahead of the rest of the field.

Hissing Sid and Prairie Rose ran as if they were joined by invisible wires. They seemed locked together, running in tandem, unable to break free from each other and Red Rag raced on and gained more ground, to finish by a good two lengths.

Our group all cheered and hugged one

another, and when we disentangled ourselves I laughed out loud to see Ned's mouth covered in Claudia's tell-tale crimson lipstick.

Apart from the glory of winning, the race was worth £70,000, and the Governor could have the whole farmhouse fitted out with the latest French ovens and walk-in jacuzzis if she wanted.

I wanted to say something original and witty to Jamie, but when I saw him, glowing with sweat and with a streak of mud down one cheek like a scar, all I managed was, "Jamie, you were brilliant! You rode like the devil!"

He put his hand briefly on my shoulder and said, "It takes one to know one."

I saw Mead turning away, looking quite sick. He must have had a lot of money on Hissing Sid to win. Well, more fool him.

Jamie was riding another race and Ned and Claudia were travelling home separately. As I waved them off in the car park, I saw Claudia's eyes fill with tears.

"It wasn't a fluke, really, Claudia," I said

kindly. "Red Rag is a real champion. He'll go from strength to strength."

"It's not that," sighed Claudia. "It's just that Florida will seem so very tame after this – even with hundreds of alligators."

I travelled back in the car with Sue and Ben, while John and another lad who was driving the horsebox set off first. Ben, Sue and I stopped at a very upmarket pub and had a delicious supper of duck with cherries and sorbets in lots of different flavours.

"That horse of ours must be favourite for the Gold Cup now," said Ben.

I thought back to the day, over a year ago, when Red Rag had arrived at the yard.

"You certainly know how to pick a winner," I said.

"And you know how to school one," said the Governor, generously.

John and the other lad were stopping at a motorway service station on the way home, where they could park the horsebox easily and grab a bite without having to leave the box unattended.

"Will I drop you off at Ned's?" asked Ben later, as we reached the outskirts of the village.

"Actually, I'd really like to say goodnight to Red Rag first," I said, so we all drove on to the farm.

"There's the horsebox," said the Governor when we drove into the yard. John was standing beside it – he must have heard us pulling up.

Ben grinned and went towards him, but John stood as if paralysed. He looked as pale as death, and his breath, making a misty cloud in the cold air, smelt old and beery.

"Has Red Rag settled in all right?" asked Ben.

"No, he... er...." said John, very quietly.

Ben looked frightened. "Well spit it out man – what?" he bellowed.

"He's gone," said John. "He's been stolen."

CHAPTER TEN

The days that followed Red Rag's disappear-ance were the worst of my life. I couldn't concentrate on anything and had to force myself to ride out and school the other horses.

I was racked with guilt. Why, oh why, hadn't I travelled home with Red Rag, instead of guzzling all that food? If I'd been as professional as an assistant trainer is meant to be, I would have stayed with the horse, even if it meant going without supper. I found it hard to talk to anyone, except to Red Rag in my head: I'm sorry Monkey, I let you down, I thought. I missed him so much I felt sick.

Even Claudia was subdued, for once. She busied herself in ringing local newspapers and radio stations and badgering them until they gave Red Rag lots of coverage.

"Put in, 'Large reward from mystery benefactor'," she told them.

Victor's wife, Wendy, was less helpful. The next time she came to the yard to see their horses – Treble Chance and Double Dividend – she wept all over the place, before saying, "I know they eat horses in France, don't they, but they don't do that sort of thing here, do they?"

The Governor marched her off to the kitchen and gave her a cup of tea and a bit of a talking-to.

John kept out of Ben's way. After Kempton, he had stopped with the lad who was driving the horsebox, not at a motorway service station for a quick bite, as he had told us on that dreadful night.

They were feeling so elated at Red Rag's win, that they stopped at a pub – off the beaten track, where we wouldn't see them – and had had a pint each. Even John wasn't stupid enough to let Red Rag be driven in a horsebox by someone who'd had too much to drink, but they'd chatted in the bar and spent too much time over their steak and kidney pies.

They'd had strict instructions only to stop at a service station, where one of them could have stayed with Red Rag at all times. The pub car park had been cramped, and some paint had been scraped off the horsebox.

The police looked at the marks carefully and made lots of notes, but we all felt they were a bit unconcerned. I suppose they had many other major crimes to investigate. Why should it feel like the end of the world to them?

The atmosphere in the yard was as heavy as lead. John, who usually whistled while he worked about the place, went about with a face like a wet Wednesday.

Lots of people rang up to offer their sympathy, as if someone had died. Jamie dropped by while I was grooming Flytrap and tilted my chin up, examining my face in the harsh, winter light.

"Becky, are you eating properly?" he said. "You're going to be no good at all to Red Rag when he comes back if you're too worn out to train him up properly."

It was the first time I'd seen a serious side to him and through my unhappiness I felt closer to him than ever before. He really cared about horses, whatever the gossip columns said about him.

Later, when I was in the kitchen, Adam Mead phoned up, and I could hear Sue's side of the conversation.

"That's very kind, Adam – the police are looking everywhere, but if I think of anything you can do..."

"He's really concerned," she said when she hung up. "I must say he sounded really interested – and that father of his even asked me in the village how we were coping. Now that's unheard of! I can't think of anything for him to do, can you, Becky?"

I was about to say, star in an advert for boil cream, but I felt too miserable even to insult Adam. It was the not knowing that was the worst thing. I thought I was coping really well, but after Red Rag had been missing for nearly two weeks, I finally cracked.

I was sitting at the breakfast table, looking at the *Racing Post,* when Ned put a boiled egg in front of me. He had drawn a funny face on it, like he used to when I was little, to cheer me up. Suddenly, everything seemed too much, and I was almost envious of my three-year-old self, when life had been so simple. Tears dropped on to the *Racing Post.*

"Now I can't read the odds for today's races," I sniffed. "Not that it matters."

Just then the phone rang. Ned answered, listened for a moment and then turned the air in the kitchen blue with a stream of colourful swearing he'd obviously been keeping bottled up since his days on the polo circuit.

"Thank heavens!" he said at last. He'd made so much noise that Claudia came rushing in, looking quite bald-faced without her make-up.

"They've found him," said Ned. "He turned up in that trainer McMurtry's field early this morning – it's only about three miles from Ben's – but McMurtry is sure it's Red Rag, he was left there just today."

I rushed off to get dressed and splash my

face with cold water. I was desperate to see how Red Rag was, and when I got to the yard the Governor greeted me with a bearhug.

"Ben and John have gone with the horse-box to fetch him now," she said. "Ben's taking John, I think, because he's been in such a state since Red Rag was taken. Poor John – I don't think he'll ever be the same."

But would Red Rag? He seemed all right when he stepped delicately down the horse-box ramp, throwing his head back as if taking in large draughts of his home air.

I rushed over to him and put my face against his neck. "It's going to be all right, Monkey," I said. "I'll never let you go again."

He'd obviously been quite well looked after and slowly my nightmare pictures of ribs sticking out and matted mane faded. But there was something different about him. Jamie came over to ride him and noticed the change as well.

"It's as if he's just arrived here for the first time again," he said. "You made him feel at home, you won his trust, and now it's as if we've gone back to square one."

He was right. Red Rag had reverted to the nervy animal he had been when he first arrived in the yard. In his stable, he didn't want anyone to come in – not even me. He would run to the back of the box.

When people walked past, he would give them a wide-eyed, wild look as if he was about to panic. He wasn't as anxious to ride out every day and seemed quite happy to stay in his stall.

When I did ride him, he was quite calm, but all the fun had gone out of him. He didn't nip at my ears or arms, almost as if he didn't trust himself not to bite if he did, and his ears stayed quite rigid, as if always on the alert. Something had happened to him, but I couldn't put my finger on what it was.

The *Racing Post* Chase at Kempton was in February.

"Have we got enough time to get him in shape for that?" I asked.

"Of course," laughed Jamie. "He's just like me – he's at his best on a racecourse. Don't worry – I'll pull out all the stops."

"It'll be like a dress rehearsal for the Gold

Cup, in March," I said.

"Don't look so worried," added Jamie. "You look like a frightened rabbit – but a very appealing one."

He put an arm roughly round my shoulders and kissed the top of my head. Before I had time to catch my breath, he laughed, and said, "Ciao, Pusscat!"

Jamie Howland kissed me! My first thought was to ring up Chrissie and tell her, but then I realised I wanted to keep it to myself. Anyway, Chrissie would only ask for details, and it was hardly the passionate kiss of the decade. But I didn't care. It was a start.

This is what taking off in a hot air balloon must be like, I said to myself as my spirits soared. If only I could find a similar magic key to help Red Rag.

CHAPTER ELEVEN

I spent as much time as I could with Red Rag over the next few weeks. Ben had to remind me that, as Assistant Trainer, I was really duty bound to help train the other horses as well, but I resented every minute I spent with them.

I was explaining this to Fay and Jessie, one Saturday evening, over a pizza.

"You're obsessed with that horse," said Fay.

"Oh, come on," said Jessie. "She's not nearly as bad as old Mead and Hissing Sid. I don't know why he doesn't have the horse in the house to live with him. God knows, the house is getting so run down that a horse moving in wouldn't make much difference.

Anyway," went on Jessie, "you've got Jamie to ride Red Rag at Kempton. Mead wanted him, but he said firmly that you'd booked him up."

"Can we come along and give you some moral support? Although, if Mead sees us cheering on Red Rag, we'll probably get the sack – which might be no bad thing. His latest economy drive includes cutting down on our rations," she added, cutting herself another wedge of pizza.

"Of course – let's make a real outing of it," I said, quashing a small voice inside that insisted I wanted to keep Jamie to myself.

So it was quite a gang that set off for Kempton; Ned and Claudia, who had Victor and Wendy in tow, Ben, Sue, John and me, with Jessie and Fay.

Red Rag seemed to have relaxed a lot more over the ten days or so leading up to the race. John, who still felt dreadful about the theft, had spent most of his spare time – and money – on him. He had bought several large padlocks, and going into his stable was like visiting Fort Knox. It had been therapeutic for both of them.

"Neither of our horses is running," said Wendy, when we'd arrived at the course, "so I want to put a whack on Red Rag to win."

"As if it's not enough you deck yourself out in new clothes – you look as if you're going to open a bridge," groaned Victor, "but you want to gamble as well."

"Oh shut up, it's only money," said Wendy. "And who was it gave you the winning numbers?"

This was a familiar argument. Apparently, Wendy had been responsible for the winning lottery ticket.

"Yes – very scientifically worked out too," said Victor, "all based on the number of times you sneezed during one of your hay fever fits."

"And you've got a nerve talking about clothes," went on Wendy. "Look at your stomach in that sheepskin coat – you look as if you've still got the sheep in there with you."

Victor snorted and handed her a bundle of notes. At least Wendy and Victor's double act helped to ease the tension and it was no time until Jamie appeared in our familiar blue and grey silks and greeted Red Rag like an old friend.

Red Rag looked quite at home, as if he was pleased to be back where he belonged and pleased, too, to be favourite. Although stories of his disappearance had done the rounds, his form was excellent and one look at him told everyone he was in superb condition.

Hissing Sid was second favourite and, I had to admit, looked pretty good as well. But we had Jamie – our not so secret weapon.

Mead and Adam had already found a good vantage point, and were waiting in silence for the race to start. Adam was biting his nails so ferociously, one by one, that I thought he would soon have to start on his toes.

Our group was in the grandstand, where we could get the best view of the finish. Ned produced a hip flask with malt whisky and passed it to Ben, who took a slug.

"Ah, that's better," he grunted. "The

nearest thing to heaven this side of the green baize door."

"I'll save myself for the Champagne," said Claudia. "Look – they're off! Hold my hand, Ned."

As usual, Red Rag shot off with the group of front runners. And as usual, I was anxious that he was keeping nothing in reserve, but Fay and Jessie both thought he was going like a dream and didn't know what I was worried about.

Sure enough, he pulled way out in front. He was a good four lengths ahead of Hissing Sid, who led the rest of the field, but then Red Rag seemed to have an extra spurt, and sped effortlessly towards the last fence.

"He's leaving poor old Sid behind," groaned Jessie, "that means prison rations for us for ages..."

We were all laughing and I was beginning to relax at last when Red Rag soared over the last fence. He was right in front of us now, and the whole grandstand suddenly erupted into a fury of cheering and clapping. The noise broke round us in thunderous waves.

And then it was as if a moment had been frozen in time. Red Rag stopped, rigid for a moment, as if in a photo finish. I felt as if I'd stopped breathing and everything around me was happening in slow motion.

Then he hooked off and raced away from the grandstand, jumped the racecourse barrier and galloped off to the centre of the course, away from the crowd. He raced as if he was being chased by mad, foaming cheetahs and Jamie could do nothing but hang on and try to slow him down.

I realised I was crying because my face was wet; I was stunned, something terrible had happened to Red Rag. When I looked at the course again, through my tears, I could see a blurred picture of Hissing Sid sprinting home easily.

Adam Mead caught my eye. He had a very strange expression on his face. Of course I could tell he was pleased and satisfied, but he also looked as if he was trying to see inside my head and read my thoughts. His father, however, just looked resigned, and limped off joylessly to the winners' enclosure.

We trooped out and waited for Jamie to come back, too numb to speak to one another. Ned produced his hip flask again, but everyone waved it away.

At last, Jamie appeared, on foot. He had left Red Rag with John. I was desperate to go and comfort both of them, but I had to see Jamie first.

"I'm sorry, I'm sorry," he kept saying.

"There was nothing you could do," I said, "he was possessed. Nobody else could have stayed on."

He flashed me a quick, grateful look and went on, "I don't know what happened. He was going so well – and then when he hooked off like that there was nothing I could do. I've never seen anything like it – if he'd kept going in the right direction, it would have been a course record!"

"It's not your fault, lad," said Ben, rubbing his hands through his hair, troubled. "Something's happened to that horse, and I doubt very much if we'll ever know what."

I looked at Ben's large, kind face,

crumpled with sadness and I promised myself that I, for one, would find out.

CHAPTER TWELVE

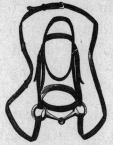

I kept telling myself that it was not as big a disaster as Red Rag being stolen. Of course, that was true. But in a way it was worse, because we had all seen just how fast Red Rag could run.

It was a real mystery. What on earth had made him hook off like that, as if someone had suddenly inserted a firework under his saddle? I spent as much time with him as I could, talking soothingly to him as I groomed him.

"Don't worry, Monkey," I said. "It was like a bad dream, but it's over now."

Jamie could throw no light on it. He'd been watching the video of the race over and over again, he said.

"I've racked my brains ever since," he said

a few days later, "but I've absolutely no idea – it was a bolt from the blue."

Claudia had her own theory. "It's all stress, darling," she told me. "Talking of which, you've been looking very pinched yourself lately."

On my next day off, she insisted on dragging me to an exclusive health club for an aromatherapy session. In case you've never come across this, you lie on a couch and are massaged with fragrant oils. Apparently I needed Clary Sage, which sounded like an old film star, but did wonders in releasing tension. Claudia tried to persuade Ben to let her rub some of the oils into Red Rag.

"At least let me hang a healing crystal in his stall," she pleaded. But Ben explained that Red Rag might swallow it.

"I don't want the vet to think I'm a complete prat," he added, which made Claudia look very hurt.

This alternative stuff about stress was all very well, but there were still the basics like feeding and exercising to be dealt with.

One Saturday afternoon I was cleaning

tack just outside Red Rag's stall. It's not the most thrilling job in the world and I had brought the radio out with me. There was football on – it was a good match and I got quite caught up in it. So when I'd finished polishing and wanted to groom Red Rag, I turned the sound up while I was working.

His ears pricked up, and he snorted.

"I quite agree," I said. "It sounds as though it should have been a penalty."

The crowd at the pitch could be heard cheering. Suddenly Red Rag began to move his legs and then thrash about as if he was going beserk. If I hadn't been there, I'm sure he would have damaged himself – he was completely in the grip of some frightening force.

It wasn't until I turned off the radio that he began to calm down. I groomed him gently, soothing him and talking to him all the time. When I felt I could safely leave him, I bent down to pick up the radio. It was then I had the flashback to that cold night in Mead's hostel, when I'd been startled by the sound of a football match. A sound that had mysteriously stopped when I went to investigate. The sound of horses panicking had been echoed by Red Rag's distress this afternoon.

If it was just a coincidence, why did I have this cold feeling running down my spine? Just as I knew I could communicate with Red Rag when I was schooling him, so he had tried to communicate something to me just then. And I owed it to him to work out what.

Very tentatively, I experimented by playing the radio near Red Rag – always in the open, where he couldn't come to any harm and never loud enough to cause a dramatic, dangerous reaction. Sure enough, each time, up went his ears and he became tense and worried.

It wasn't just football. Any loud noise, but particularly the sound of crowds cheering – startled and unsettled him.

Before I did anything else, I had to persuade Ben to listen to my theories – and Jamie, too. So I borrowed tape recorders from Ned and Sue and recorded bits of football matches – just the crowd noises of cheering and shouting.

Then I asked Ben and Jamie to come up on to the gallops, and gave them a tape recorder each, primed to play at full volume.

"Switch them on as soon as you think we're within earshot," I told them. "They'll be very loud, but don't turn them down at all."

"Couldn't we just pass an orange along under our chins, instead?" said Jamie, teasing me, and Ben looked at me as if I'd gone completely mad. But then they could see just how serious I was and agreed to enter into the spirit of the experiment.

It was a magical January day and the last patches of frost were just going, when I mounted Red Rag and started off up the gallops. I deliberately rode as calmly as a scientist conducting an experiment.

Red Rag loved galloping up this stretch, which he'd come to think of as home. It would take a lot to unsettle him up here. As we reached the figures of Ben and Jamie, they had turned on the tape recorders and a raucous din sailed slowly but surely towards us, shattering the peace of the cold air.

For a split second, everything seemed to go into slow motion as Red Rag hesitated. Then he careered away from the noise, like a bat out of Hell, forcing me to hang on for dear life. It reminded me of the time he'd been frightened by Glendower, when he was newly arrived at the yard. But there was even more urgency about his bolt this time. I knew him well enough, by now, to know he was terrified.

I've no idea how far we galloped, but at last he slowed down and I managed to calm him, catch my own breath and canter back until we met Ben and Jamie, who'd been running after us.

"Are you all right, Becky?" called Ben.

"Fine," I gasped. "Let's get Red Rag back to the yard – I think he's OK – and I'll explain the point of all that."

We gave Red Rag to John and went into the kitchen where the Governor was waiting to hear what had happened.

"Wait till I get us all some tea," she said, putting a plate of newly grilled potato cakes, dripping in butter, on the table.

I told them about Red Rag's reaction to the football match on the radio earlier, and explained my theory about crowds cheering.

"But what are you saying?" said Jamie, leaning so far forward that I felt I could have dived into his eyes, they were such a singing, clear blue.

"I'm saying something happened – was done, rather – to Red Rag when he was stolen," I said.

Then I told them what had happened at Mead's yard – the noises coming from the quarantine yard, and his over-the-top reaction. I hadn't mentioned it before. For some reason, it had seemed unprofessional to do so, and I had been so keen to appear professional in my first real job.

"There's obviously some connection," said Jamie. "Look, I know there's something fishy about Mead's yard, but I'm over there quite often, riding out, and I never saw hide nor hair of Red Rag during that time he was missing."

"But did you ever go near the quarantine yard?" I asked.

"No, I didn't, it's true," said Jamie, wiping butter off his chin. "Your friend Jessie – the one who looks and acts like a Shetland pony, warned me about it – as well as Mead, of course..."

"And Mead was so concerned when Red Rag went missing," said the Governor. "I remember bumping into him in the village, and he was more sympathetic than I've ever seen him."

"Huh!" I said. Not a very intelligent or helpful comment, I admit, but it made me feel better. "He could be pretending to be helpful to cover things up," I pondered.

"It's all very well," said Ben, "but we have absolutely no proof that Mead was involved."

"At least now we know what throws Red Rag – and nearly ended up by him throwing Jamie and Becky," he added ruefully. "We also know that horse can run like the wind –

or a hurricane. But where does that leave us? Somehow, I don't think we can persuade the whole meeting at Cheltenham to watch in silence..."

And then it came to me. The idea was so obvious that I felt as if a light bulb had lit up on top of my head, like in a comic. But I had to convince them.

"The race meeting can't watch in silence," I said. "But Red Rag can run in silence."

Jamie understood first and reached over and grabbed my hand.

"Sorry to be so thick," said Ben, "but is there any chance of letting us in on this?"

"We plug his ears," I said. "We do it as often as we can between now and the Gold Cup, to get him used to it. And we put him in blinkers – and a hood. You know it's quite common for horses to run in hoods. It should deaden the noise enough."

"Ear plugs and a hood," repeated Ben. "Belt and braces..."

"I wouldn't go as far as that," laughed Jamie. "But I think it's a brilliant idea. Look, I'm going to Mead's yard tomorrow. It won't hurt if I let drop – quite casually – that you've no idea what made Red Rag bolt, but you think he's recovered. That should lull them into a false sense of security. Meanwhile, you experiment with plugging his ears. Is your vet discreet?"

"Dick Shannon?" said Ben. "I've known him years – I was at school with him."

"Well ask his advice," said Jamie. "There's probably some special kind of ear plugs you can use – cotton wool might come out half way round the course."

It all seemed to be falling into place. At least now there was something I could do and I could hardly wait to start experimenting with Red Rag and noise control.

Jamie offered to run me home. In the car, I said, "Look, Jamie, I know you're incredibly busy working," (I stopped myself from adding 'and trying to snatch the odd night in'). "Are you sure you've got time to get to the bottom of – you know, Red Rag and everything?"

We were just pulling up at the cottage. Jamie swivelled round in his seat and pushed the hair back from my face.

"We're in this together now, Pusscat," he said. "For as long as it takes."

"And what's put that huge smile on your face?" asked Claudia when I walked into the cottage.

CHAPTER THIRTEEN

We set to in earnest to try and see how Red Rag ran with ear plugs, a hood and blinkers. At first, when we kitted him up with all the gear, he looked at me as if to say, "Is this some kind of joke? What are you doing to me?"

"You'll soon forget you're wearing all this, Monkey," I said. "When you're racing, you won't have to worry about anything except winning."

I felt guilty that I was neglecting the other horses, but told myself it would even out after the Gold Cup. Then I thought of a way round this. In the evenings, when Red Rag was stabled, I wrote reports for our owners on their horses – detailed reports – on Ben's computer, outlining their progress, condition, even diet.

"Hey, this is terrific!" said Claudia, one Saturday morning when she got her first report on Florida's Hopes. "And will I get these when I go home?"

"Of course you will," I said. "They'll be even more useful then."

"I'm already starting to get separation anxiety," said Claudia.

"What's that?" asked Ned. "Is it that feeling you get when you're making hollandaise sauce and you think the egg and butter are going to separate?"

"No," said Claudia seriously. "It's when it's nearly time to go home and you have a sinking feeling – more like when your sponge cake doesn't rise."

I went out into the garden, tactfully I thought, and threw a stick for Shelley, but soon Ned called me in: "Telephone for you. It's Jamie."

"Hi, Jamie," I said. "How're things?"

"Becky," he said and my stomach turned over the way it always did when he said my name. "I've got something to tell you and I don't want to say it over the phone. Can we meet tonight – perhaps for a drink?"

I kept my voice quite calm and casual as I replied, "Of course. Why not come here? Ned and Claudia are out, ticking off another country restaurant on Claudia's list."

Later, I soaked in a deep bath with some of Claudia's oils – lime and tangerine – in it. I stayed in until my fingers were as wrinkled as prunes and I smelt like a fruit salad. Then I pulled on my favourite jeans and a scarlet polo neck and brushed my hair until it gleamed.

Perhaps this was the night Jamie was going to tell me how he felt about me – that he was fed up with bimbos – and appreciated everything we had in common, our love of horses and racing. That he hadn't known how he really felt about me until he had seen Red Rag bolting and galloping off with me in deadly danger, over the frosty hills...

Even I could see that my fantasy was getting a bit Mills and Boon and I switched on the radio for the football results and made myself a good, strong cup of tea.

Soon, I heard Jamie's MG drawing up and I went out to meet him. He jumped out, tossing his dark hair out of his eyes.

"Beer?" I asked; he nodded and followed me into the kitchen.

"I didn't really want to say this over the phone," he began and my heart missed a beat, "but it's about Mead."

Oh well. I could always dream.

"I've been at Mead's yard quite a bit recently," went on Jamie, "schooling a couple of horses. I made a point of trying to investigate the quarantine yard."

"And?" I interrupted.

"Well, no luck there," said Jamie. "It's wide open – no secrecy at all. I asked the lads – and your friends Jessie and Fay, of course – why horses were kept there, but they just said for the usual reasons. If a horse has a temperature or a cold, it would be put in there to stop it transmitting the virus to the other horses. Mead is just understandably anxious that people don't go in there or the virus could be easily spread.

"But I did learn something quite useful, I

think," Jamie went on. "It seems that Mead's been putting on huge bets for Hissing Sid to win the Gold Cup. He's convinced that Red Rag – who was the only real threat – is totally out of it and this is his big chance to make a killing. All the lads say he's desperate for money – he's often late with their wages and he's cutting corners all over the place."

I remembered Jessie complaining about the quality of the food.

"But Hissing Sid's been picking up prize money," I said. I was enjoying this intimate chat and wanted to prolong it for as long as possible.

"Apparently Mead is in real financial trouble and needs a massive win to wipe it all out," said Jamie. "That's why the Gold Cup is so vital to him. I've always known he was a gambler, but I didn't know what a strong grip it had on him. It partly explains why Adam's life's been such Hell since his mother left. I really think he hates his father."

"It makes me realise how lucky I've been, being brought up by Ned," I began, settling down for a cosy talk about relationships. But Jamie sprang to his feet and looked at his shiny Rolex watch.

"I should be somewhere else," he said. "I just wanted to fill you in, and I wondered – are you free on Wednesday afternoon, because Mead and Adam are away for a day's racing."

"Yes..." I said, trying to see the connection.

"Good," Jamie went on, "because I think we should pay Mead's yard a visit. Uninvited – but then they're not known for their hospitality, are they?"

Meanwhile, Ben had told Dick Shannon, the vet, about Red Rag's problem with noise, and he'd come up with ear plugs that seemed to do the trick. We subjected Red Rag to lots of trials on the gallops, with horrendous noise roaring out at him from ghetto-blasters, and he stayed as calm as anything, which is more than I did.

Jamie was involved in these trials, of course, and Red Rag grew used to being ridden by him in a hood that covered his ears and face and blinkers over his eyes. It was not unusual for horses to run wearing this gear, but I couldn't help feeling sorry for him. Why shouldn't he race with his mane catching the light and the crowd seeing just how handsome he was? It made me even more furious at whoever had conditioned him like this and more determined, if possible, that he should win.

Claudia was getting caught up in the excitement and was putting a whack of money on Red Rag to win.

"Just think," she said over supper one evening, "I could buy a dear little cottage with my winnings – I saw one for sale in the village."

I looked at Ned's face, but whatever he was feeling, it was well hidden. He might as well have been wearing a hood and blinkers himself. I laughed out loud at the ridiculous picture this conjured up and Claudia said, "I'm glad to see you unwinding, Becky. Now you and I must have a serious talk about what we're going to wear to Cheltenham."

Ned took his chance to grab his coat and take Shelley for a walk.

When Wednesday came, Jamie drove me over to Mead's yard. Mead and Adam had shared a horse transporter with another trainer for the racing and Jamie parked beside it now. When I climbed out, I noticed that the horsebox had paint scraped off the sides. Not only that, but there were odd smudges of bluish-grey paint on the bare patches.

"Look, Jamie," I said. "Blue and grey – Mainwaring racing colours. Don't you remember our horsebox had paint scraped off after Red Rag was stolen? It was such a narrow space where John had parked it, the two boxes could easily have scraped against each other."

"Mmm," said Jamie. "It could be coincidence – after all, you're always going to the same meetings. Let's try and find something more concrete. Perhaps there'll be vet's notes or something in the office and we can work out what happened to poor old Red Rag while he was missing."

We went round to the office, meeting Fay on the way.

"Everyone else is away and I'm in charge," she said. "And before you ask, I haven't seen you. You know what they say about me – Fay by name, fey by nature. I hardly notice a thing that goes on around me."

Jamie grinned and grabbed her hand and kissed it, and jealousy filled me, right down to my boots.

"Mead told me he's coming back about six-thirty," went on Fay.

It was already five o'clock, so we let ourselves into the office. It wasn't locked as the safe was in the house, further protected by the burglar alarm – and we were hardly likely to see a wall chart showing 'steps towards sabotaging Red Rag'.

"Let's be systematic about this," said Jamie. "I'll look through his desk drawers, and you deal with the in-trays on that table."

Mead appeared to be very disorganised

and the in-trays held teetering piles of papers. There were old betting slips and training notes, but nothing dramatic. I also found a receipt from an off-licence; he may have been cutting down on food, but his drink intake didn't seem to be suffering. And this was a man who never entertained. It was obviously a sign of stress.

We had to make sure to put everything back in exactly the same place.

"I don't think he'd notice," I said. "It's all in such a mess."

"We can't take that chance," said Jamie. "We want him to feel quite secure about Hissing Sid's chances – he must feel that we've stopped worrying about Red Rag and what caused him to bolt."

Before we knew it, it was a quarter to six, and we had still found nothing that backed up our suspicions. We were running out of time, when Jamie spotted a brown envelope that had been lying on Mead's desk all through our frantic search.

"Look!" said Jamie. "It's addressed to Sam O'Brien."

Everyone in the racing world had heard of Sam O'Brien. He was a bookie and a flamboyant character with suits as loud as his patter.

"We're going to have to open this," said Jamie.

"But it's so well stuck down," I whispered – I don't know why, as Mead wasn't around. "There's no way we can seal it again."

"There's a packet of brown envelopes, just the same as this one, in the desk," said Jamie. "And it's obviously been typed on that old typewriter over there. We'll type a new one – you start typing and I'll look at the contents."

I put an envelope in the old typewriter and Jamie emptied the old one and passed it to me to copy. I had just finished the name – the typewriter kept sticking, and I was used to the elegance of Ben's word processor – when Jamie shouted.

"He's in deeper than we thought! In here are the deeds of Mead's stable, house and land – worth a cool £600,000 – and a cheque for £250,000. If Hissing Sid loses, he stands to lose everything. I haven't got time to read all the detail, but there's a letter mentioning huge sums Mead owes O'Brien – and it seems he's using all his property as collateral on Hissing Sid winning at Cheltenham. He's going for broke."

"But it doesn't help us with Red Rag," I said.

"No, but Mead is sure Hissing Sid is going to win. Ben was saying Red Rag and Hissing Sid are joint favourite, right?"

I nodded.

"Well, Mead knows that Red Rag isn't going to win. And there's only one way he can know that..."

Just then the door burst open and Fay rushed in.

"It's Mead," she shouted, "he's back early. I'll think of something to get him into the house, but you'd better hurry..." and she ran out again.

I carried on typing, but the keys kept sticking and my fingers were hot and sweaty. At last I finished the address, and quickly stuffed the old envelope into my pocket.

Jamie was just putting the papers in the new envelope, when we heard the back door of the office opening.

We were standing beside a window, and the way the back door opened meant we were hidden from sight by a huge old filing cabinet. There was no way we could cross to the front door without being seen.

Jamie wrenched open the window until it started to squeak. I looked at the space and thought, I'll never get through that, but Jamie had already grabbed my arm and was pulling me through with him. I imagined us getting stuck and Mead coming round and seeing four legs sticking out into the room and had an hysterical urge to giggle.

But when I heard Mead's rasping cough, I sobered up. It all happened very quickly, and the next thing I knew we were lying in what had been a flower bed, and was now a weed bed, under the window.

"I just hope he doesn't notice the window's open and look out," breathed Jamie into my ear.

We could hear Mead rootling about with

papers and then there was the screech of chair legs on linoleum, as if he'd pulled out the chair at the desk to sit down.

"Come on," whispered Jamie, urgently.

I'd been enjoying lying so close to him that I could sense him breathing and smell his skin. But our mission was accomplished and we crawled off through the weeds together, like a couple of naughty children.

CHAPTER FOURTEEN

Red Rag had never been running better. We didn't know exactly what had happened to him while he was missing, but we worked hard to regain his trust and he was repaying us in the only way he knew.

He'd grown really used to running in, what the Governor called, his Hallowe'en get-up. And I took extra time to talk to him and reassure him after each ride.

I would say things like, "Now, now, Monkey, you feel really secure in your new gear," over and over again, very calmly, like a hypnotist. I knew things were going well when he started nipping playfully at me again.

I resented the time I had to spend on paperwork and spent so many extra hours with Red Rag – who would really always be Monkey to me – that, if Ben had been paying me overtime, I would have bankrupted him.

Since we'd found the envelope for the bookie in Mead's office, Jamie and I felt even more sure that he was behind Red Rag's disappearance, but we had absolutely no proof. We consoled ourselves by remembering that he knew nothing about our noise experiments, and was in for a surprise.

As the Gold Cup grew nearer, the tension mounted. We knew we had to keep Red Rag in tip-top condition and I was experienced enough now to know just how much could go wrong. Jamie told me about a horse he knew which was tied up on the side of his stable while they were mucking him out. He'd managed to rub his nose against the door, which had a sharp metal edge. Before anyone realised what was happening, he'd cut his mouth and it was too sore to put a bit in.

"He missed the vital race he was being trained up for," said Jamie.

"Any more cheery stories?" I asked.

"I want you to watch every step that

horse takes from now on," said Ben, when the Cup was only five days away.

"Last year my friend Harry's horse was up for the Cup and he was walking him through a gateway back from the gallops – a path he took every single day – when somehow he managed to work an old, rusty nail right into his hoof and was out of action for weeks."

I began to think that anything could happen – there were so many freak accidents. Everyone was keyed up and showing it in different ways. I wished that there was some sort of race before the Gold Cup so that we could have a dress rehearsal with the new hood, but there was nothing suitable.

The Governor scrubbed Red Rag's boots meticulously every time he wore them, so that no dry mud could cause a rub on his legs. When she wasn't doing that, she was cooking furiously. Soon she'd filled her freezer and was starting to stock ours.

Claudia stared at the latest delivery of venison pies that had arrived on our kitchen table and said, "I told Sue I never mix starch and protein. I tried to explain that I follow the Hay diet, but she just laughed and said so did the horses..."

"Don't worry, I'll eat them," said Ned. When he was nervous, he ate vast amounts, but never seemed to gain a centimetre.

I couldn't sleep at night, but tossed and turned worrying about boot-rub and blisters. I had a series of really vivid dreams, in which awful things happened to Red Rag. In one, he literally turned to stone in the middle of the Gold Cup and Jamie was left sitting on a statue.

The next night, I dreamt the starter pistol went and all the horses raced off, except Red Rag, who was rooted to the spot.

Then I had a dreadful nightmare, where we opened the horsebox at Cheltenham to find Red Rag dead in the back. I woke up screaming from that one, and Claudia rushed in. After that, she made me drink a mug of camomile tea before bed every night. I did it just to please her and, whether it was coincidence or not, the dreams stopped.

As the race approached, I had never seen

Ben so serious.

"I'm trusting you, Becky," he said. "As Assistant Trainer, you must make sure that horse doesn't tread on a rock and bruise his sole." It was all very well, but I felt no one cared if my soul was bruised.

Jamie came over two days before the race for a last workout on the gallops, and even he seemed more tense than I'd ever seen him.

"He's going like a dream," he told me afterwards, "but I can't help thinking that he hasn't run with his ear plugs and hood in front of a live crowd, all shouting and waving their arms about. Ghetto-blasters are all very well, but they're not the same."

"Well, we'll soon find out," I said. We were taking Red Rag to Cheltenham the next day, to let him settle in.

"I'm having an early night tonight," said Jamie.

"Don't let the press find out," I smiled, "or your reputation will be ruined."

We had decided to take Red Rag to Cheltenham the day before the race because he was still a little nervy and unpredictable and we wanted to steep him in the atmosphere of the festival before his big race. Although the stabling was some distance from the actual racecourse, a lot of the cheering could be heard there, and we felt sure this would acclimatise him and help him relax into the general atmosphere.

We were taking our own transport. Ben didn't want to share with another racing yard in case there was a bug or virus going about. A horse can pick up something like that and, within twenty-four hours, its performance can go right down the pan. We were leaving nothing to chance.

"Ned and I will see you tomorrow," said Claudia as I set off on the Wednesday morning.

"I expect you're off shopping for a new outfit today," I said automatically. But she gave me a huge hug and said, "I haven't given it a thought."

I suddenly realised how much warmth

Claudia had brought into my life – and I did not just mean the way she kept stoking the fires, trying, in vain, to recreate a Florida climate.

"Cashmere is as much a necessity here as toothpaste," she'd said one day to Ned, who looked totally puzzled.

The Governor had pulled out all the stops in the appearance stakes and was wearing a black and white dog-tooth suit and had packed a scarlet hat and scarf for the next day.

I was wearing cream, stretch cords and my pink cashmere sweater and was taking a wool suit for the racing.

We'd already worked Red Rag for the final time on the gallops and we set off with plenty of time to spare.

"Let's just get there, then we can relax and have a sandwich," said Ben. "I don't want to take any risks by parking the horsebox."

So we actually got to Cheltenham before the day's racing had started, and who should we bump into as soon as we got down from the horsebox, but Adam Mead.

"Hi!" he called. "Great to see you, Becky."

I could tell he really meant it. Isn't it just incredibly *annoying* when the wrong person fancies you?

"We've been here for ages – oh, a good hour and a half," Adam went on in his plodding way. "You know how the old man's paranoid about time – so why don't I help you unpack?"

I suppose I'm a bit of a sucker, but I really felt sorry for Adam – especially as I knew his inheritance was about to disappear when Red Rag romped home. I kept thinking how ghastly it was for him to have Mead for a father. It almost explained how horrendously Adam had turned out. Only almost – there was a lot of natural lack of charm in there too. So I agreed and soon everyone was unpacking something; feed, hay, tack and it wasn't till much later, when I had time to catch my breath, that I thought I should check that the bridle had arrived safely at the tack room.

One of the lads I had got to know said, "It's here, lass, don't you be worrying – that Adam Mead dropped it off. He seemed more concerned about your tack than about his own, but then you're a lot prettier than that old bear of a father of his."

I ignored this and went off, quite relieved, to check that Red Rag was safely stabled. Then I changed into my suit and met up with Sue and Ben to enjoy the day's racing.

Jamie was racing later and I wanted to get a good vantage point. He came second, and was obviously on terrific form.

"The only thing wrong with that," I said when Ben and Sue were saying how well he'd ridden, "is that he was wearing the wrong colours. As Claudia would say, 'Blue and grey are absolutely his colours!'"

Ben knew loads of people there and every time he introduced me as his assistant trainer, I glowed with pride. There was a photographer from some glossy magazine who snapped us – with Ben in the middle, his arms round Sue and me. I thought of the surprise Claudia would have when she flicked through the magazine in the hairdresser's.

As the day wore on, I began to see why Ben had said the Cheltenham Festival was special. It had an atmosphere you could slice through with a whip.

After the day's racing, we went back to the small hotel we were booked into and had the human equivalent of a rub down and bran mash – hot baths and a drink. Ben had arranged to have dinner with some other trainers, and I felt a bit nervous, as if I was an impostor and one of them would rumble me.

"Here we are," said Ben, when we had walked to the restaurant. It had small, thick glass windows like the bottoms of bottles and lots of dark wood like something out of Dickens. The Snaffle Bit – the owner is a retired trainer – I've known him for years."

Inside, there was a round table near a fire, with about six ruddy-faced men sitting at it. As Ben introduced me to them, one by one, I wondered what on earth we would talk about and suddenly felt quite homesick.

But I needn't have worried. Not surprisingly, they all wanted to talk about horses –

form, breeding, who won what – and I soon found I was in my element, quoting winners and times to my heart's content.

"Where did you find her?" I overheard a plump man called Billy asking Ben. "Not only does she look like an angel, but she seems to have swallowed a dictionary of breeding as well."

I'm afraid I ignored the sexist remark and basked in the fact that they all treated me as a professional. To think that only a matter of months before I had been at school. Why was it I couldn't remember any French grammar, but I could remember who won the Tetley Chase three years ago?

We finished supper with special coffees with cream floating thickly on top. I don't know what was in them, but as soon as I'd finished mine I felt as if I could hardly keep my eyes open.

"Time to turn in, I think," said the Governor and we walked through the dark streets to our hotel.

I washed quickly and slid between the crisp, clean sheets. I was quite sure that I wouldn't sleep a wink, as I switched off the light and snuggled down. But the next thing I knew, the Governor was knocking on my door, calling, "It's six o'clock – we're meeting Jamie at seven. Are you awake, Becky?"

I sat bolt upright in the dark room and hugged my knees. It had come at last. The Gold Cup was within our grasp.

CHAPTER FIFTEEN

I pulled on my cords and threw open the bedroom window. It was still dark but the air was cold and crisp and smelt of Cox's apples.

"Come on, Becky," said Ben downstairs. "You must have some breakfast – we'll all be so busy who knows when we'll next snatch a bite."

I poured myself a cup of tea and tried to eat a piece of toast, but my mouth was so dry that it just went round and round like a dish-cloth in a tumble drier.

It was a relief to rush off and saddle up Red Rag, who telegraphed his pleasure at seeing me with his ears. I found it almost hard to see him objectively now, although I knew he was in superb condition. But some of the lads who were already up and about at that hour were very reassuring.

"Good luck," said a small Irish lad, patting Red Rag on the side, "I've put all me wages on you, so I have – now don't be telling my boss."

"It's the big day at last," said Jamie, coming up and putting a hand on my shoulder. "I'm going to take him out for a little spin, so look out his hood and EP's."

We'd started calling the ear plugs EP's, because we didn't want people to know exactly what we were up to. It was vital that Mead thought Red Rag wasn't a threat – that he would panic again at the crowd noise. If he didn't believe this, he might even try to sabotage Red Rag again.

"See if you can rustle me up a bacon sandwich for when I get back," said Jamie, as I gave him a leg-up and he trotted off in the morning mist.

I was waiting when they came back, with a flask of coffee and a sandwich just the way Jamie liked it – heavy on the bacon, with just a smear of horseradish. I handed these to him and took Red Rag away to wash him off. I dried him meticulously and checked him over. By the time I had rugged him and given him his feed, I had to admit that I had never seen him looking better.

"This is our big day, Monkey," I said to him. "Don't let me down now."

Jamie was draining the flask of coffee when I caught up with him.

"How did he go?" I asked.

"Like the wind," replied Jamie. "He's had a good pipe opener and galloped really well. We'll just have to keep our fingers crossed."

There was a lull now until about two o'clock when I would get the tack organised. Ben and Sue were there to keep an eye on Red Rag and I wasn't meeting Ned and Claudia until the race itself. I was as restless as a new colt but Jamie seemed to pick up my mood.

"Ben and I are going to walk the course," he said. "Are you coming?"

I didn't need to be asked twice. We set off together and Jamie told me the tactics he was proposing to use. It was my idea of heaven –

Jamie, technical racing chat, a beautiful spring morning and the promise of all our hopes coming to a climax before long.

"D'you think I should stay on the inner?" Jamie asked Ben. He meant the inner side of the rails.

"Now what would you say, Becky?" Ben asked me.

I could tell he wanted to see how I was shaping up, and I thought carefully about my answer.

"Well," I said seriously, looking at the turf, "I'd say the going was good to soft. It'll soon be churned up by hooves, so the second circuit will be heavier going than the first. So going on the outer would mean getting a bit better ground.

"But knowing Red Rag as I do," I went on, "I'd say keep him on the inner. He likes to be a front runner. And – because it's a left-handed track – he'll end up not quite so close to the stands."

"That's my girl!" said Ben, slapping me on the back. "Well thought out – and, just for the record, I agree!"

The fences at Cheltenham are well known for being stiff and walking the course brought home to me just how up and down it is, with the finish up a very long hill.

"I feel as if I've run the race myself," I said. "What's that whirring noise?"

It was helicopters, landing nearby.

"One of those'll be the Queen Mum," said Ben.

I had worked towards the race for so long, that I hadn't thought about the aftermath. But Cheltenham was a village of grand tents and terribly smart people, and suddenly the thought of winning the Gold Cup and being the focus of all that publicity made me feel quite shy. And I'm not the retiring type.

When we headed back to the yard I felt much more settled.

"I've got to dash," said Jamie. He raced off, tossing his dark hair from his forehead and shouting back, "See you in the winners' enclosure Pusscat!"

It was about half-past one when I decided it was time to sort out the tack, so I went off to the tack room. There was absolutely no sign of Red Rag's bridle. I checked everywhere and asked everyone in sight if they'd seen it, but there was no trace. I began to think I was going mad. I searched the whole stable area and I was getting that prickling feeling under my arms that comes when I'm really frantic with worry.

Ben was nowhere to be seen – and I knew he trusted me to sort out all the tack.

"I should have just sat beside the tack, instead of gallivanting off with Jamie," I told myself sternly. "Now, pull yourself together – there's bound to be a simple explanation. Probably the Governor's put it in the horse-box or something."

I walked up the steps of the horsebox and towards the side door. There was a funny noise coming from inside that I couldn't identify and a strange smell – a sort of den-tist's smell, as I described it later.

When I pushed open the door, the first thing I saw was Red Rag's bridle, lying across one of the chests that we pack our tack in. Next to the bridle, catching the light, was a small, very shiny steel saw. Beside it, lay a shooting stick. The last time I'd seen one of these, Mead had been using it. I filed this away in my mind to discuss with Jamie later.

I was flooded with relief to find the bridle but then the prickly feeling in my underarms started again. I wondered what on earth was going on. Who'd put that saw there and what had they been up to?

I was walking up the horsebox, juggling all these thoughts in my mind, when suddenly, from nowhere it seemed, something soft and moist was thrust over my face. It was like being in a ghost train, and suddenly being ambushed by something totally unexpected and frightening. Except, of course, in a ghost train you expect frights, but you don't in your own horsebox.

Everything went black and when I woke up my head was muzzy and I felt as if I was swimming up through treacle. My hands were tied behind my back, my legs were tied together; but the worst thing was the tape across my mouth – I was completely helpless.

I had no idea what time it was, or how long I'd been out of things. I could see the bridle had gone and I prayed that someone had taken it to the valets' room. It was like being in a nightmare. Had the race been run? I had no way of knowing.

I pulled myself up into a sitting position, using muscles I didn't know I had, and wriggled along to the driver's seat. I felt so ill that all I wanted to do was get out and breathe some fresh air. But although there were people about, I couldn't scream.

I slumped forwards, my head hitting the horn. Automatically, I pulled my head away, but then I realised that was stupid. It's your only chance, I thought, and I put it back down and left it there. The horn blared out for what seemed like hours, although I expect it was only really about five minutes.

At last, a lorry driver came rushing up to the horsebox and began banging his fist against the door, shouting, "Hey! What the hell are you up to? You'll frighten the horses!"

He climbed up and peered through the window as I turned my bleary, tear-stained face with the tape across it towards him. He tried to open the door, but it was well and truly locked.

"All right, lass, hold on!" he shouted in quite a different tone of voice and rushed off.

A few minutes later he was back, clutching a huge spanner and my eyes widened in fear.

"Keep your head down," shouted the lorry driver and he smashed the window. Very carefully, he put his huge, tattooed hand through the hole and opened the door. He climbed up and, quite tenderly for such a huge, butch man, pushed my hair back from my face.

"This'll only hurt for a moment," he said, and he pulled the tape off my face – very fast, as if it was a plaster covering a cut on my knee.

He untied my hands and legs and I staggered down from the horsebox, trying to stretch out my stiffened limbs. My head still felt as if it was full of cotton wool, but I took a deep breath of fresh air, and turned to my rescuer. "Thank you, thank you, Oh help! What time is it? Has the race started?"

"Search me, love," he said. "I'm the delivery man – and knight in shining armour!" he added with a grin.

I took to my heels and ran fast in the direction of the course, with the lorry driver shouting after me, "Hey! Shouldn't you be taking it easy?"

As I ran, thoughts raced through my mind. I remembered the saw beside Red Rag's bit. Had someone been tampering with it?

I passed a bookie friend of Ben's and he called, "You're cutting it a bit fine, aren't you? They're nearly off."

I was flooded with panic and for a moment I felt as if I was in one of my nightmares, rooted to the ground. I ran as if I was wading through treacle, sweat trickling down my back. There was no way I could check Red Rag's bit before the race. Jamie would need even more luck than we'd thought.

But there was no more time to worry. Just

ahead of me, a shout went up: "They're off!"

I ran until I found a vantage point where I could see the end of the race. I looked around but there was no sign of anyone I knew. Ben, Sue, Claudia and Ned must be wondering what on earth had happened to me.

I strained my eyes to see over the people in front of me as the horses thundered past. Out in front was the unmistakable flash of blue and grey silk. Some horse I didn't recognise was a whisker behind and then, a couple of lengths behind, came Hissing Sid.

The horses were nearing the grandstand for the second time and I knew that this was Red Rag's big test. He was pulling away from the horse behind, and the crowd was roaring and waving.

The last fence was about twenty lengths away and I could see very clearly now. Jamie's jaw was tensed and his face was grimly determined as Red Rag sailed over the fence, his hooves barely touching the ground.

"Come on, come on, you can do it," I breathed, digging my nails into the palms of my hands.

My eyes were riveted on Jamie, when his arms suddenly flew outwards.

I grabbed some binoculars from the man standing next to me. No! Oh no! I could see now that the bit had come away from Red Rag's mouth. Jamie would have no control at all! In a flash, I knew what had happened. Someone had sawn through the bit – just enough to weaken it, so that it would snap under pressure.

We thought we'd got everything under control, but we had been done at the last moment.

As I watched in horror, Red Rag began to drift away from the fence. It was a repeat of Kempton but this time, instead of hooking off he would just drift away. I couldn't look. Jamie was hanging on valiantly, trying to steer Red Rag, but without the bit he was like a rudderless ship.

The second horse had fallen right back now, and Hissing Sid was coming up fast behind. If he'd been on Red Rag's inside, it would all have been over.

But he wasn't. He was on the outside. He ran along neck-and-neck with Red Rag and between them Jamie and Hissing Sid kept Red Rag on course as he jumped the final fence.

The two horses thundered up the finishing straight and now all Red Rag had to do was keep running straight ahead. He couldn't drift off, because Hissing Sid was still at his side. But towards the finish, this obviously annoyed Red Rag. Whether he could see Hissing Sid in spite of his hood and blinkers, or whether he just sensed him and his mighty vibrations, we'll never know. But he knew his natural position was out in front. So he gave a final spurt, or Jamie managed to squeeze an extra burst of speed from him, and he raced home to win the Gold Cup by a head.

He'd won! My Monkey – winner of the Gold Cup! It was all over and I wasn't even embarrassed then that I was surrounded by complete strangers, all staring at me, as I shook with sobs.

"There, there, dear," said a woman in a fur coat. "Have you lost a lot of money?"

It was all too complicated to explain, so I gratefully accepted a tissue and stumbled off to meet Ben and Jamie. John had also seen what had happened, of course, and had raced down with a halter for Red Rag, who had luckily pulled up with the other horses.

"Becky!" exclaimed Ben. "Where the hell have you been?"

When I saw his familiar, crumpled face, I burst into tears.

"In the horsebox," I started, "I was... I was... "

"Slow down, girl," said Ben, putting an arm round my shoulders. "We've got all the time in the world, now."

"I couldn't help it," I stammered. "It wasn't my fault... How did you find the bridle?" I finished.

"The bridle? I think John picked it up from the tack room."

"I don't ever want another ride like that," said Jamie, dismounting then wiping the sweat and dirt off his face with his sleeve.

It took Claudia, coming up and throwing her arms round everyone, to remind us that, in spite of everything, we had actually won the Gold Cup.

"Although, watching, I must admit I didn't really understand your tactics," she said to Jamie, who grinned weakly.

"Yes, they were rather unusual, Claudia," he admitted, as he left to weigh in.

Ben and I looked at the bit. It was obvious that it had been sawn nearly in half, but whoever had done it, it hadn't mattered, although it could so easily have meant disaster. If it had snapped halfway round the course, I was sure all would have been lost.

We all walked down to the winners' enclosure and everyone we passed thumped Ben on the back and shouted their good wishes – a lot of them unprintable! I recognised most of the trainers from the night before and they greeted me, too, like an old friend.

Ben and the Governor were an incredibly popular couple – known for Ben's jokes and Sue's ability to conjure up miraculous amounts of food and drink at the drop of a riding hat. Ben had battled away for ages, hoping to prove himself, and although years of hard graft had gone into it, it suddenly looked as if, overnight, he had won one of the biggest races in the world.

I knew I had to tell Ned and Claudia about what happened in the horsebox, but I was all right, and Red Rag was all right. It was like waking up from a nightmare.

"Oh Ben, I'm so happy," I said, as my feelings ricocheted from gloom to ecstasy. "No one can ever take this away from us."

I wouldn't have been quite so happy if I'd known that someone was about to try.

CHAPTER SIXTEEN

In the winners' enclosure the Governor adjusted her scarlet hat and took Ben's arm.

"Have you heard the one about the woman who married a fat old dairy farmer and he turned into a top trainer?" she said to Ben.

"You ain't seen nothing yet," he replied, glowing with pride.

"Isn't it just wonderful to see a happily-married couple?" said Claudia to Ned, who just grunted. He had made a point of taking me aside and telling me how proud he was of me.

"And you don't think I'd be better going off to college and doing something useful?" I couldn't resist asking.

"I know enough about life to know you

mustn't look a gift horse in the mouth, if you'll pardon the pun," said Ned. "Ben tells me you've got a real gift for training horses. Your parents would have been so proud of you today, Becky."

I had to pretend I had a smut in my eye and fiddled with my crumpled tissue.

And suddenly, there it was in the flesh – or precious metal, rather – the Gold Cup itself.

Ben went up to take it amidst loud applause. We were all beginning to relax – the mystery of the bit would be unravelled in good time – but we had serious celebrating to look forward to. The second and third prizes were about to be handed out. Mead was waiting, like a man about to mount the steps of the guillotine, and Jamie and I knew why he looked so ghastly. His world had crashed around him – he had staked everything on Hissing Sid to win, and he'd come in second. In Mead's case, there really were no prizes for coming second.

He looked green – I could just imagine Claudia describing him as eau-de-nil and saying what a lovely shade he was for silk under-wear.

Before Mead had a chance to collect the second prize, Adam, his chin thrust out displaying a fine crop of boils, strode over to him and shouted, "They must have cheated, they just must have cheated. There must be some way they've cheated," he went on.

"Keep your voice down," said Mead. "You're making a fool of yourself."

"You don't understand," Adam ranted on. "They've cheated, I tell you!"

"Look," said Mead at last, "if you don't shut up, I'm warning you, I don't know what I'll do..."

He raised his stick in the air and waved it at Adam, as if he was putting a spell on him.

Red Rag suddenly reared up and tried to pull away from John who was holding him, dragging him to the other side of the winners' enclosure. He looked quite mad, with nostrils flaring, and the spectators looked terrified, but John managed to calm him down. For a moment, you could have heard a horseshoe drop. Then Adam just looked resigned and the prizegiving carried on.

Afterwards, we all piled into the car – apart from Jamie, who was racing the next day – and set off for home. John would bring Red Rag home safely, we all knew. He'd lay down his life for that horse, now.

In the dark, womb-like security of the car, I felt I could tell the others exactly what had happened to me.

"This isn't a prank or high spirits we're dealing with," said Ned. "This is serious. I'm going to call the police right away."

I begged Ned not to. I didn't want anything to spoil the pleasure of our win that evening. He agreed to put it off till the morning.

"I think they'll be interested to see that bit," said Ben.

I was ready with lots of theories of my own but I must have dropped off because the next thing I knew, we were pulling up at the cottage and the only place I wanted to be was in my own bed.

I was too tired to wash properly and brushed my teeth on automatic pilot. I certainly couldn't be bothered with camomile tea; now all the excitement was over, I was beginning to feel a bit fuzzy, like I had in the horsebox.

But I should have listened to Claudia, and drunk it, because that night I had a real 18-rated, full-colour nightmare. I was trapped in a horsebox, and someone was barring the exit. I knew that if I didn't get out, something dreadful would happen. The face of the person trapping me was blurred and it was up to me to bring it into focus.

In the morning, Ned told me he had heard me shouting, "It's no use – I can't do it, no matter how much I twiddle the knobs."

CHAPTER SEVENTEEN

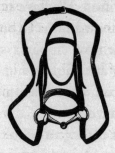

Jamie called the next morning and we arranged to meet at the pub in the village. It was wonderful to be able to tell him everything that had happened.

"I don't know about these things," he said when I described the pad or whatever being thrust into my face, "but it sounds like chloroform. Thank God it wasn't anything worse."

"Whatever it was," I reasoned, "it put me in the dark – and we're still totally in the dark, Jamie. I've no idea who took the bit and sawed through it."

"That's true," said Jamie, draining his glass of Guinness, "but remember how Red Rag reacted when Mead lifted his shooting stick. It was as if he recognised it – and the horse was terrified. We have no evidence at all, but you must admit it all seems to point to Mead. Look how embarrassed he was at Adam drawing attention to him at the prize-giving. Mind you, if I'd been hit by a plague of boils, I'd have kept in the background myself without having to be told."

"Ned is contacting the police – about my attack," I said.

"That's all very well," said Jamie, "and they'll probably be very methodical and painstaking about the whole thing but take forever. I think we should do some detective work of our own."

"Can't we just relax for a bit and bask in the glory?" I asked, feebly.

"Whoever's done this isn't going to stop here," said Jamie. "And if it is Mead, well he must be really desperate – he's seen every-thing go down the chute."

So we arranged to visit Mead's yard again the next day, when our mole, Fay, assured us they would be out racing.

The first thing we saw when we drove up to Mead's yard was a garish FOR SALE sign.

I couldn't help feeling sad; Mead had built up the yard over the years and now it was all being sold because of his gambling, which was really an illness – an addiction that I knew from Ned could bring a whole family terrible unhappiness.

"This is no time to be soft-hearted," said Jamie. "Hi, Jessie – how're things?"

"Dismal," said Jessie, coming out into the yard to greet us. "We've all been sacked – know of any jobs going?"

"I think the Mainwarings are expanding," I said. "They've had lots of enquiries on the strength of the Gold Cup. But you'd probably hate working there – the Governor never stops cooking and practically force-feeds the staff with huge meals. The sort of things you hate – steak and kidney puddings, apple dumplings – that sort of thing."

Jessie's eyes widened. "Do you really think I'd have a chance?" she asked.

"I'll put in a word for you, if you like," I said.

"Right – business," said Jamie. "Look, Becky, you start off in the quarantine yard and I'll take the main yard. Now we don't know what we're looking for, we're just having a good search – anything may turn out to be a clue to solving the whole thing."

I strode off to the quarantine yard and went over it with a fine tooth comb. It was a bit difficult, not knowing what I was looking for, but at least I felt I was doing something concrete.

I came across nothing of interest and decided to have a look in the tack room. I was sure I would recognise the small hack saw – it was imprinted on my brain – and if I found it among Mead's tack, that would be a pretty hefty clue. And just think how pleased Jamie would be with me!

I was looking through the tack, when a voice behind me said coldly, "And just what the hell d'you think you're doing?"

I froze. I couldn't believe I'd been caught red-handed like this, but I thought on my feet and managed a smile before I swung round and said, "Adam – hi!"

I was so relieved that it wasn't Mead himself, that I managed to relax. "I left my crash hat behind and I was just wondering if somebody had put it in here – for safe keeping," I finished lamely. "I see the yard's up for sale," I went on, gabbling as always when I'm nervous.

"Are you thinking of moving on? I hope you're not thinking of moving out of the district – I always think of you as a kind of fixture." Like a septic tank, I thought to myself.

I gave what I hoped was an appealing smile and it seemed to work because Adam said, "Do you really think so, Becky? Well, actually, I am thinking of training – taking out a licence and training myself. I really enjoy it.

"I haven't seen your hat," he went on. "Sorry. Look, you're getting quite a reputation for schooling and I think you're a brilliant rider."

I couldn't help feeling just a bit flattered, in spite of myself.

"I know you're brilliant at setting up

jumps," Adam was saying, "and I've set up some show jumps at the outdoor school, but I'm not sure I've got them right. I'm really keen to maximise Hissing Sid's potential. Would you mind – if you could spare just five minutes – coming up to the outdoor school with me, because I'd like you to set up a line of fences that *you* feel would help him become a bit more athletic."

I wondered if a sharp kick in the shins would help Adam become more athletic but, under the circumstances, I could hardly say no, could I? Anyway, I knew the outdoor school was only about a mile away and I didn't think it would take long. Luckily, Jamie was keeping well out of sight.

Perhaps I could winkle some information about his father out of Adam. So I agreed and we walked up the drive to Adam's car – the grotmobile as Jessie called it.

Jessie saw us and rushed out calling, like somebody in a bad amateur drama group. "Becky – I'm so glad you could make it. D' you want some tea?"

"No thanks," I called back. "I looked

where you suggested, but I couldn't find that crash hat and now I'm off to the outdoor school with Adam."

I spoke very clearly, as if I was speaking to an idiot, but I knew Jessie would tell Jamie where we were going.

When we were in the car, Adam said, "I'm sorry about my performance at the prize-giving the other day."

"Oh, don't mention it," I said. "We were all a bit tense."

"It's just that I wanted to win that race more than anything I've ever wanted," said Adam, his knuckles tightening on the driving wheel. "I'm afraid I overreacted. I would like us to see more of each other," he went on. "After all, we do have a lot in common. There's horses, and..."

I could feel him racking his brains for another shared interest.

"And then there's horses," I said and he laughed in a loud, neighing sort of way, showing yellowish teeth.

There was a tape lying on the dashboard, with a white label stuck on it.

A-ha! I thought, this must be Adam's taste in music. I bet he's plugged into something really juvenile. And I squinted at the writing on the label.

Crowd noise, it said. I thought that was strange but I forgot about it then, because I was trying to think how I could pick his brains about his father. Perhaps I could find out if Mead had ever been violent to Adam, but it was hard to think of a light, jokey way of phrasing, "Did your father ever beat you up?"

He was beginning to drive quite fast. I had taken off my denim jacket before I got into the car, and I turned to toss it on to the back seat. Lying there was a pig-poker. What would Adam want with a pig-poker? They only kept horses. The shape of it reminded me of something and I suddenly remembered Mead's shooting stick.

A pig-poker. A tape of crowd noise.

I gave Adam a sidelong glance. It was so unlikely that he could have engineered such a subtle plan to terrorise Red Rag. He had always been so eager to help. Even at

Cheltenham he'd helped unload our tack.

I felt as if someone had drenched me in cold water.

Adam had helped unload our tack. The valets knew him and wouldn't have been at all suspicious of him. He would have had plenty of time to mess about with the tack. It would have been a piece of cake for him to saw through the bit. I felt sick now, as other thoughts crowded in.

I remembered how Adam had never stood up for his father when the stable girls and lads ran him down. It was in his interest for us all to think that his own father was up to something - at his own yard – so that Adam could quietly get on with his nasty, underhand plans.

When Red Rag reared up, in the winners' enclosure, it wasn't because he was frightened of Mead. It was because he had been broken down and terrified – cold-bloodedly – by Adam, using a pig-poker and some crowd noise.

I turned my head and our eyes met. In that instant, he could tell that I knew.

I began to sweat. Adam speeded up and I realised we'd passed the entrance to the outdoor school and were headed off towards the next village. I looked at Adam's face. It wore the same expression that I'd seen at Kempton – a weird look that made the hairs on the back of my neck stand up.

I was more frightened than I had ever been in my life. Where was he taking me?

CHAPTER EIGHTEEN

"Your Dad didn't steal Red Rag, did he?" I asked Adam as we hurtled round the country lanes.

"The old man?" he said, sounding quite surprised. "He hasn't got the brains."

"But why was he so paranoid about the quarantine yard?" I couldn't help asking.

"He was paranoid about everything," said Adam. "He was paranoid about us only using two sheets of lavatory paper, so he could spend the saving on his gambling habit. I'm afraid he's all washed up now," said Adam.

His voice had gone deeper and he seemed to think he was sharing some sort of secret with me. I honestly think he expected me to be impressed by the way he'd handled his revolting scheme.

He thinks he's in a film, I thought. He probably thinks I'm in it, too – and I'm quite dispensable. I wonder what part of the plot he's pencilled in for me?

I tried desperately not to panic, and kept on talking.

"I feel sorry for your father," I said.

"Don't waste your pity," said Adam. "He's beyond help. But I'm not – yet. The Gold Cup was my one chance to break free of him. I knew he'd staked everything on it – all that was meant to come to me. If we had lost, he would have drunk himself to death and I would have lost everything that was meant to be mine – the house, the business, everything."

"What do you mean 'if we had lost'?" I said. "You did lose."

"Well no, actually," said Adam. "Very soon the Mainwarings should be getting quite an interesting phone call from the Jockey Club."

"What do you mean?" I asked, alarm

beginning to show in my voice.

"On the day before the race," said Adam, "I took a horse out on the gallops long enough to simulate a race. Then I took a sample of blood and added a drug – a banned drug that improves performance. It was a piece of cake to swap this sample for Red Rag's after the race – the security at that course stinks. Do you want to know how I did that?"

He was still eager to impress me.

"I can't imagine how you could have," I said, seeing the outdoor school flash past the car window and trying to keep the panic from my voice. He was wondering whether to tell me, or keep the details to himself, so I said, "I don't believe you. You're making all this up."

That was all it took.

"I know the vet who was in charge at Cheltenham that day," said Adam. "I practised his handwriting, so that, when I wrote Red Rag's name and the date on the sample I substituted, it looked really authentic."

"Gosh, Adam," I said, trying not to look appalled.

"And – as an assistant trainer," he said, "as you yourself know, Becky, it doesn't seem strange if you're in the stable area after a race – checking up on your horse, or just passing through.

"When the vet had taken Red Rag's sample and was bent over with his back turned, checking his legs, it was very easy to switch them.

"Any minute now, the samples will be analysed, and your bionic horse – which looked so charming running in its pixie hood – will be disqualified."

I stared at Adam and he looked quite mad.

"I'm impressed," I said. "But where are we going now?"

"I've got an old barn out in the wilds I use for things like, well, special stabling," he leered. "And you can hole up there until the word comes through from the stewards. You see, I knew you'd work out what had happened. We're very alike, you and I. You'll be quite safe for a few hours.

"Once Red Rag is disqualified, that'll be it. And if you tell them what I've just told you, they'll just think it's desperation. The desperation of a cheat." He laughed.

I'd had enough and, now I knew I was being kidnapped, I had nothing to lose. Adam had become desperate himself, I could tell. His plan for me was ridiculous.

Although I was terrified, I couldn't help saying, "How desperate would someone have to be to give a horse shocks with a pig-poker? Desperate and cowardly."

Of course he didn't deny it and I began to think I'd said too much and he would stop the car and beat me up.

I felt sick, but then I caught a glimpse of something red out of the wing mirror. I turned my head and saw Jamie's MG coming after us.

"Oh look," said Adam, who had seen it at the same moment. "It's lover boy on his red charger. Don't tell me you find him attractive. He's so – obvious. Well, don't worry, we'll soon leave him behind."

He put his foot flat down on the accelerator and we raced forward. Jamie was managing to keep up, but Adam was driving like a maniac.

We must have been doing about 90 along those narrow lanes, when he took a corner too fast, the car's nearside wheels went up on to a bank and it turned over.

I landed on top of Adam with a crack that sounded like a stick of rock breaking – in fact it was my arm. He knocked his head on the dashboard and lay there, unconscious.

I heard the screech of wheels behind us and Jamie jumped from his car.

"Becky! Are you all right? Becky?" he shouted frantically.

Dazed, I managed to call back. "I think my arm's broken, but Adam's been knocked out."

"I'm going to try and get you both out of there," called Jamie. "The car might go up in flames at any moment."

I managed to manoeuvre myself through the door and climbed out on to the side of the car. Jamie pulled Adam – who was a dead weight – out of the same door.

"Mead didn't do it," I gasped, when he had lain Adam on the ground at a safe distance from the car. "It was Adam – he's all eaten up with bitterness, it's awful."

"First things first," said Jamie, and he went off to call an ambulance. He's got a car phone, which makes him sound a bit flash, but he needs it so that trainers and people can contact him wherever he is. It's not as if he has a desk job.

While we were waiting for the ambulance to arrive, I told him everything Adam had told me.

"It all makes sense in a horrible sort of way," he said. "If Mead was really trying to sabotage us, he would surely have tried to hide it behind a more charming face."

"But what about the blood sample, Jamie?" I said. "How are we going to prove that?"

The ambulance arrived, by which time Adam was already coming back to life, and the paramedics said they thought his outlook was pretty good.

"All main functions working well," was how they put it. They wanted me to go into hospital, too, but I was desperate to see Ben and tell him everything and persuaded them Jamie would take me in his car.

This brilliant paramedic woman strapped up my arm and I promised to turn up at outpatients later that day.

"You're sure you're not in pain?" said Jamie, as he helped me into his car.

I looked into his deep blue eyes and, lying, I said, "Not any more."

CHAPTER NINETEEN

Jamie drove me to the farm and we sat Ben and the Governor down at the kitchen table and told them everything.

"I'm so sorry, Ben," I finished. "After all your hard work – will they ever believe that the blood samples were switched? Why should they?"

Ben started laughing and I thought at first it was hysteria.

Then he said, "Look, there's been so much funny business surrounding this race – from Red Rag being stolen to rumours of other horses being certs to win, and crazy betting on the joint favourite – that I didn't take any chances. I got my own vet, Dick Shannon, to take a sample from Red Rag after the race, under the stewards' supervision. And that's in the stewards' safe – quite separate from the sample Adam switched."

"Gosh, Ben," I said, "that's impressive. You deserve your success."

"Oh, you know what they say about me," said Ben, rubbing his head. "Belt and braces – I don't take any chances."

"I didn't marry him for his looks, you know," said the Governor.

"Terrific!" said Jamie, getting to his feet. "Now I think I should take Becky to the hospital to get her arm in plaster, and then I'll let Ned know what's happening."

He grinned and added: "After he's listened to all this, he'll probably feel like getting plastered as well."

In fact Ned and Claudia were very good about everything. Ned had contacted a detective after I'd been attacked in the horsebox, and this chap took statements from me and Jamie, Ben and Sue and Jessie – he practically took one from Shelley.

It was ironic that the sample Adam had substituted was the main piece of evidence against him – because Ben's was as right as rain. Adam's dreams of being a top trainer went up in smoke and his father's life was left in tatters.

The last we heard was that Adam's case was coming up before the court in August and Mead had sold everything and was going off to live alone in a cottage in the south of Ireland.

"I hope he finds some peace there," said Claudia when she heard. "I understand how he feels – I don't think I want to go back to the social madness of Florida; all those drinks parties, all those plastic surgeons and palm readers. I've been thinking, and I've decided I want to spend my winnings from the Gold Cup on that cottage in the village."

"I don't want you to buy that cottage," said Ned.

I froze. Ned wasn't one to beat about the bush, but I'd never known him be cruel.

Claudia went pale and her hands, with

their fuchsia polished nails, gripped the table.

"I don't want you to," went on Ned, "because I want you to stay here. Now that Becky's made a life for herself, I've realised how much I like having you around. What on earth would I do if you left?"

"You want me to organise your social life, your wardrobe, that kind of thing?" said Claudia.

"I want you to marry me, you fool," said Ned. "And it's going to take a lot more potions and crystals than you've got to change my mind."

"I'm very sorry, Claudia," I said, "but once Ned's made his mind up, that's it."

I went over and kissed her and added, "And I couldn't be happier. You've become part of the family."

I thought this was a good time to leave them together, so I went out into the garden where Shelley bounded up to me.

"Never mind, old dog," I said, "you'll always love me, won't you?"

I felt so happy for Ned and Claudia, so why did I feel just a tiny bit jealous?

I gave Chrissie a ring and told her the glad tidings and, as usual, she brought me down to earth. "Yuk!" she said. "You mean they're getting married – and are actually going to *do* it? But they're really old. That's disgusting!"

Of course, I couldn't ride with my arm in plaster but I managed to do some office work, typing out the owners' reports with one hand. There was a terrific atmosphere at the farm.

Red Rag seemed to have settled down again and was becoming one of the most famous horses in the country. Although I couldn't ride, I visited him every day and talked to him.

"Just you wait until I've got this stupid plaster off, Monkey, and we'll be off up the gallops."

Obviously, I was very proud of his success, but what was more important to me was that he was happy. I only had to look at his ears to know that.

Ben had taken on two new horses and Jessie had been hired to help. At last the Governor had someone who was on the same wavelength about cooking and they had long, deeply serious conversations about the proportion of kidney in a steak and kidney pudding or just how chewy meringues should be.

Fay had gone off to the States to work for a friend of Claudia's and bombarded us with fey postcards. As far as it was possible to tell, she was having a great time.

Another reason I spent so much time at the farm was to give Ned and Claudia lots of time together. It would be nice, I thought, if life worked out like the end of all those Shakespeare comedies we did for English GCSE, with everyone pairing off neatly into happy couples. But there didn't seem much chance of that as far as I was concerned.

Chrissie kept suggesting that we go to discos in the village but I only wanted to go if a certain person would be there.

Actually, I hadn't seen Jamie for a bit, but quite early one May morning, I was staring out of the office window at the blossom on

Sue's apple trees, when the door opened and in he came.

He'd come to get the measure of one of the new horses.

"I do miss riding, Jamie," I said, wistfully. "You don't know how lucky you are."

He came over and looked at my plaster cast, which had gathered a good collection of signatures – from the village butcher's to Claudia's large scrawl in violet ink.

"Did you know violet is a healing colour?" I gabbled, suddenly nervous at his closeness.

"Can I sign?" asked Jamie and I handed him a pen from my desk. *Kiss me!* he wrote.

"Really?" I asked. I was about to laugh but then I looked up and saw his face.

"Becky," said Jamie, looking serious for a moment, "you must know how I feel about you."

"You are joking," I said. "I've always thought you liked me in the way I like – well, Shelley."

Jamie threw back his head and roared with laughter.

"I'm sorry to disappoint you," he said, "but I've never fancied Shelley. I fancied you, however, the minute I met you," he went on.

"You toe-rag!" I screeched. "You could have given me *some* sort of clue."

"Look, I've had enough talk about clues," said Jamie. "In fact I've had enough talk."

He put his arms round me – very carefully, because of my plaster, but there was nothing at all careful about his kiss.

You're not going to believe this, because I know I rabbit on a bit, but when he kissed me again and I kissed him back, I somehow knew I wouldn't feel like talking for a very long time.

GINNY ELLIOT first started riding when she was three years old. Her mother used to collect her from school on horseback, leading another horse for Ginny so they could ride back home together.

By the age of seventeen, Ginny had won the Junior European Championships on *Dubonnet*, a horse that had been bought at a Cornish cattle market for £35. This was just the start of many major successes including wins at Burghley, Badminton and both the European and World Championships, on such well-known horses as *Master Craftsman* and *Welton Houdini*. She was also a member of the silver medal-winning Olympic team at Los Angeles in 1984 and Seoul in 1988.

Ginny is currently the Jump Team Coordinator for the British Three Day Event Team and lives in Oxfordshire with her husband, Michael.